The Bu[...] Baths Murders

Gordon Thorburn

FIDO PUBLISHING

© Gordon Thorburn

ISBN 0 9527638 6 9

The rights of Gordon Thorburn as author of this work
have been asserted by him in accordance with the
Copyright, Designs and Patents Act 1993

All rights reserved. No part of this book may be
reproduced, stored in a retrieval system or transmitted in
any form or by any means without prior permission from
the publisher

British Library Cataloguing in Publication Data:
a catalogue record for this book is available from the
British Library

Designed and typeset by Richard Shiner
dick@shinerlite.demon.co.uk
Typeset in Times New Roman

Printed by MFP Design and Print, Manchester M32 0JT
info@mfpprint.demon.co.uk

Published by Fido Publishing, Buxton SK17 9DX
fido@thorburnicus.demon.co.uk

*Cover photograph from the Board Collection, Buxton Museum
and Art Gallery. Reproduced by kind permission of Derbyshire
County Council Libraries and Museums Service*

ACKNOWLEDGEMENTS

My dear wife Sue, when reading the first draft of this book, said she thought that I shouldn't try and upset people. For instance, the bit at the beginning about the king and the white mare was rather too strong. I said 'What do you mean? That's what they used to do!'
    She said 'Oh, I assumed you'd made it up.'
    'Made it up?' I said. 'How could I make up something like that?'
    My wife gave me what they used to call an old-fashioned look, which is why I am explaining here that I didn't make up that bit about the king's initiation, nor any of the historical background. The story of The Buxton Baths Murders might be entirely fictional but there are many debts in the detail, especially to Mike Langham and Colin Wells of Buxton and to Keith Matthews, Tom Ikins, Mireille Busby and others of the internet wells-and-spas cognoscenti (wells-and-spas@mailbase.ac.uk).
    Mike Langham's excellent books, written with Colin Wells, include A History of the Baths at Buxton and, with Mike Bentley, Buxton from the Board Collection (of photographs).

    Thanks to them all, and my wife,
    from Gordon Thorburn, 1st June 2000.

By the same Author

THE APPLEBY RAI - travelling people
on a thousand year journey
Photographs by John Baxter

VILLAGE CRICKET, the genuine article
Photographs by John Baxter

43 UNSPORTING MOMENTS
Illustrations by Paul Davies

AQUAE ARNEMETIAE, EX ROMA, EX ROMA, VIA, VIA, LONGA EST, VIA LONGA EST.

"Buxton is a long way from Rome."

Marching song of the VI Legion

PROLOGUE

"HAIL! I'm Severus Crispus."

"Hail! I'm Horatius Cocles."

"Any relation to the man who kept the bridge?"

"Doubt it. Please, sit. You're obviously new and from the south, so welcome to Aquae Arnemetiae and her baths. You won't find me keeping any bridges here, mainly because there aren't any. We have to wait for the rain to stop because, if it does ever, the river might go down far enough to ford."

"It can't be as bad as that, surely?"

"It's easy to tell when people have been at Aquae for any length of time. They go pale, like the British. You'll soon lose your sunny complexion here, I can tell you. If it's not raining today, it probably was yesterday and it's definitely going to rain tomorrow although, funnily enough, the sun always shines for a funeral. I've noticed that particularly, because we've been having a few extra of those lately."

"Extra funerals?"

"Indeed so, Severus Crispus. Murders. Very mysterious. The victims are always men, could be any class but they all have two things in common. One is the baths."

"What? These baths?"

"Just so. Citizens who had been to the baths and were walking home, or slaves of the baths who were out on an errand. The first one was a centurion, a Cappadocian from Trapezus. He was on leave from duty in the north with the Sixth, so obviously he would be desperate for a thorough cleansing session in the baths, that is assuming a Cappadocian could ever be cleansed. Well, the British got him on the way back to the villa he was staying in. We don't have a castella here any more, so if we get any army chaps we have to put them up in civilised quarters, whether they're used to it or not. Anyway, that was months ago, and there've been at least four more since then."

"The British got him? Four?"

"Five with the centurion. Seems like it would have to be the British, and several of them. Five murders looks like too much work for one man."

"Or woman."

"Or woman. Mind you, I'll say this for the British. Nothing they do could surprise me. Nothing. Have you heard what they used to get up to when they had a new king? You know, their equivalent to a coronation? Where we would make a little wreath thing out of a few laurel leaves and ensure that everybody got pissed, they start off with the poor sod having to mate with a horse. No, I tell you, it's right. If this chap is to be king, they find him a white mare, not necessarily the most attractive one in town, and he has to give it the benefit. Then, they have a big song and dance about killing this poor old mare, and they cut her up and put all the meat and blood into the biggest pan they've got, and the king has to step in and splash it all over. Then, they cook it up and eat it! Have you ever heard anything like that? Can you imagine our revered Emperor...I tell you, my friend, never underestimate the British. They are capable of absolutely anything."

"What's the other thing they have in common?"

"What?"

"You said the murders had two things in common. The baths, and..."

"The way of doing. Whoever the killers are, they seem to be mistrustful of any one particular method and so always employ three. The victim is strangled, then clouted with a blunt instrument or stabbed and, just in case, left in the river where he can drown if he's not properly dead."

"Good heavens. I've heard of shooting arrows or throwing spears into people being crucified, but that's only two methods. Three does seem rather excessive."

"The gossip is that it's a religious thing, the old British threefold death which the druids used to perform. Sort of sacrifice to their gods. But quite frankly I don't see what good a Cappadocian centurion is going to do as a sacrifice to the British gods. Probably put them right off, if you ask me. Probably have a negative effect. Don't you go sacrificing that smelly Cappadocian bastard to us, they'll say. We'd rather have a billy goat any day of the week."

"Isn't Arnemetia a god, or goddess, rather? Goddess of the water we're bathing in? It isn't her they're sacrificing to?"

"Shouldn't think so. She's a healer. People make wooden statues of her and throw them in her pool, or they make clay models of the bits of their bodies they want cured and put them where the spring can flow over them. My wife said she was going to make a clay model of my private parts and see what Arnemetia could do about our sex life. However, enough of that, Severus Crispus, and changing the subject from the potential sacrifice of those who use the public baths, what's the latest from Rome, assuming that's where you've been?"

"Well, the Roman gossip is about religion too. They say that Emperor Constantine is going to move the capital to the east and turn everybody Christian. He's supposed to be considering three sites, Sardica, Troy and Byzantium, with Byzantium the odds-on favourite."

"Well, he can say goodbye to Britain, then. Rome's far enough away as it is, in thought and distance. If the Emperor's going to look to the east, we shall have to look to our backs. It's not twenty years since his father had to come over to give the Picts a good walloping. The minute they hear about Byzantium, they'll be down here and giving us constant sunshine for weeks."

"He died at Eburacum, didn't he? The Emperor's father? How far's that from here?"

"Correct. Died after repelling the filthy barbarian hordes. The baths will be the safest place when they invade the next time. They'll never come anywhere near hot water in case it weakens their spirit, or dilutes their woad or something. And if you want to go to Eburacum before the Picts get to it, it'll be about sixty or seventy thousand paces in a straight line, or call it a good three days' march not quite in a straight line. Two ways you can go. The roads are probably better through Mancunium and Cambodunum, but it's a very stiff walk over the hills. It means going down from here and then you have to reclimb all that height. I'd go Legiolium, Calcaria if I was you."

"I don't know if I'll get the time for quite a while. I'm here to do a detailed survey on the lead mining."

"Best of fortune, my friend. On your own? Well, I hope you won't have to meet too many of the miners. Of course, here in Aquae it's relatively civilised. Most of the local riffraff speak Latin. But the miners! Wild men of the hills, they are. Our local garrison commander, when we had one, wouldn't even use them for emptying the latrines, despite their undoubted skill with a shovel."

"Oh, no, Horatius, I don't think I shall need to talk to any miners. I just need the numbers, you know, output, costs, that sort of thing. This move of the imperial capital is going to prove very expensive and the emperor has decided that he needs to know precisely how wealthy he is."

"If he's relying on the lead mines for funds he won't get very far. He'll get more money if he prays for it to fall out of the sky. Maybe he should try it on his new god, Christus or whoever he is."

"That's why the emperor's going east. He wants to avoid a confrontation with Rome. Everyone I know in Rome is still faithful to the old religion, if they have one."

"Old? It's not that old. Not compared to the ones with human sacrifices and the threefold death."

"Well, whatever, in any case the educated Roman classes don't go for this Christianity."

"Same here. I don't think it's got much of a hold anywhere in Britain except Londinium and they always were ones for the latest fads and fancies. If it catches on around this part of the world I'll be very surprised. Up here in the cold wet hills they like their religion strong and hot. They don't want all this carry on with forgiveness and meekness. The druids might have been rubbed out but that doesn't mean the old gods and the old beliefs have gone as well. Does it?"

"No, I suppose you're right. Anyway, it wasn't so long ago we were burning Christians alive and watching them try to run faster than a leopard. Or putting them down the mines, come to that. I don't suppose there's a circus in Aquae, is there?"

"Circus? You'd be hard put to find a horse that can gallop, except away from the next British king. No, there's no circus. Nearest one used to be Danum but I don't know if there's much on these days. Shortage of good horses, and a shortage of good criminals to fight each other. At least in the good old days you could always rely on some keen young army officer to go out and catch a few rebel tribesmen to give us a bit of fun. Now everywhere's so peaceful, the only blood that's spilt is at the doctor's. Or on the way home from here."

"Is that true about the murders? You're not having me on."

"True as I sit here. In fact, I think I've sat here long enough. Time for a scrape."

"Is there a decent taberna we can go to, after we've been scraped and washed? Does wine get as far north as this?"

"Come to my house, Severus. I have some very good wine from Gaul. I used to be there, in Bononia, met my wife there as a matter of fact, and I still have a few contacts. I generally send some wool cloth and salt pork in return."

"Pork? What, are you a farmer, Horatius?"

"Sort of. Keep a few pigs, a few chickens, and these dreadful scrawny things that pass for sheep around here. I think any Roman living in Aquae would find it hard to keep up a standard of living without some land to grow his leeks and onions and rear his own meat. Quite honestly, trying to buy decent stuff from the British is almost impossible. Fine if you want to eat oats all the time, or things made from those parts of animals we throw away - mixed with oats, naturally - but if you want proper food, you have to grow it yourself. Look, you must come back for dinner. I'll go on ahead and you turn up when you're ready, Severus Crispus."

"Thank you very much, Horatius Cocles. I'll maybe linger here a little, then have a look around. How do I find your place?"

"Out of here, follow the path to the east about 200 paces, then take the path to the south, up the hill, through the woods, and we're on the very top of the hill. You can't miss it. See you later. And stop staring at that girl like that. You'll go blind."

"Well, she is rather...goodbye! See you later. You, girl, come here! Bring a jug of hot water. Good. Now, I see that the upper part of your garment is exceptionally well filled at the front. Are you going to show me what's filling it?"

"No, sir, I am not."

"What? You're a slave. I command you. Show me!"

"Pardon me, sir, but I am no slave. I am called Nemesia and I am the daughter of an important official although I cannot tell you which one."

"Oh yes, and I'm the Queen of the Iceni."

"It's true. My father is a very strict man. He will allow no airs and graces. 'We are all citizens of Rome!' he says, five times a day. So my brothers have been made to join the army as common legionaries, and I am to work in the public baths for a year, a slave to all but a few intents and purposes."

"Then I must say I am sorry to be so rude and peremptory."

"I quite understand. I understand much better than you might think. I have seen my reflection. I know that the gods have been good to me and that I am very beautiful. My body awakes great stirrings in men and envy in women. I am very proud of my body and I like to choose occasionally someone other than myself to look at it. So, although I will not accede to your commands, this does not mean I won't agree to a polite request. You can come with me now if you like. There is no-one in the frigidarium. We could go there."

"The frigidarium? Won't it be...?"

"I don't think so, Severus Crispus. Already I can see you are looking forward to raising the temperature with me."

....

"When did you tell him to come, Horatius?"

"I just said, dear wife, when he was ready. By that, obviously, I meant don't be too long. Maybe an hour or so. I never imagined he would be all this time. He surely cannot be so rude to someone who offers him hospitality."

"Surely not. It is impossible. Something has happened. We must send out our people to look for him. Let us pray they don't find him face down in the river."

CHAPTER ONE

4th June 1944.

Dear Mrs Mercer, I hope you will forgive me writing to you like this. I'm not really supposed to do it but I'm in hospital in Rangoon, the war's over for me, and I so much want to tell you about the bravery of your husband. I expect you had the usual 'Killed in action' from the War Office, and I know the CO wrote you a good letter. There was even a rumour that Major General Wingate himself had written to you, but they can't tell you what really happened. I can, because I was there.

On that night, because of losses, we were a makeshift amalgamation of different bits of B Company, an extempore platoon, you might say. We were myself as officer, a section sergeant, a corporal but no lance corporal, and six private soldiers. We had been through quite a lot of fighting and were on our way back to base, at night, in skirmish order. Of course we were old hands. We knew how to move silently and we knew that if we didn't, we were asking for it. Most of us had also acquired the ability to see, or rather sense, the presence of another human being on the other side of the wall of darkness. It's a funny thing but after you have been in the jungle a while, you are almost better off in the dark than you are in the daytime. In the light, you stare at the undergrowth and try to see through it and into it, try to catch a movement or a shape with your eyes. At night, you just let your other senses work and, when they're attuned, as ours were, it's like having your own personal RADAR set or crystal ball.

With this sort of confidence and carefulness, you can perhaps imagine our astonishment when a sub-machine gun suddenly rattled off from very near-by. Several men fell. The rest dived for the floor. In the silence that followed we could hear the sounds of someone running away.

I made an audit of our new estate. Our Sergeant killed. Three men wounded seriously, one lightly. Four unhurt, including your husband, whom I think I can now call Private J G Mercer VC, can't I? I expect you will have been to see the King by the time you get this.

Anyway, as I'm sure everyone knows, the practice in the Burmese jungle is to leave behind anyone who's hurt badly enough to slow down the rest. We give him food and water and a loaded gun. If he improves his condition, he can try to get home and some have done so. If the Japs find him, he keeps the last bullet for himself.

Quite honestly, with only five of us fit to move, we felt in a quandary about leaving three wounded. The Japs knew where we were. They would come back to finish our wounded lads off. When they'd done that, they would be not very far away from the rest of us when they set out in pursuit. We talked about it. Another option was to set a trap around our wounded, wait for the Japs to come, and ambush them. The Japs would guess that's what we might do. They might leave us alone for days, and nights, and we only had very limited rations. It was very difficult, Mrs Mercer, to decide what was best, and certainly I wasn't going to take the decision on my own with such experienced men around me.

The wounded lads wanted to be dug in so they could fight longer, which was fine except we were low on ammunition. How much should be left with them and how much for the others who had a better chance of getting back?

We were talking or rather whispering in such keen debate that nobody noticed that Private Mercer had disappeared. When we did realise, we sat in absolute silence. None of us knew if the Japs had somehow sneaked up and taken him, or if he'd gone off on his own for some mad reason. Mrs Mercer, I have to tell you, at that point I believed your husband was already dead. I believed we were surrounded by Japanese who would come in with knives and take us one by one. That was my firm understanding of the situation.

After about ten minutes of sitting without a sound, we heard three pistol shots in quick succession, followed by a short burst of automatic fire, followed by a scream, followed by silence. I don't think I have ever listened to such silence as we did then. I imagine that in death, or in outer space, there is silence like that but the difference is, there you have no-one to listen to it. We listened, with a mixture of resignation and high tension in our hearts, to the most complete and utter absence of noise, a calm which must surely be broken suddenly by a storm.

Of one thing we were all sure. Whatever was going on, Private Mercer was the cause of it.

We waited perhaps another fifteen minutes before we heard anything more. It was a rustling in the bushes, a deliberate rustling it must have been because we never made a sound normally and the Japs certainly wouldn't. Then a voice was hissing. It said 'Sir! Lieutenant Mycock, sir! It's Mercer!' He came in among us on his hands and knees and collapsed to the ground.

He died as dawn was breaking. We buried him and Sergeant Askham, and we said this prayer over them. 'Forasmuch as it hath pleased Almighty God of his great mercy to take unto himself the souls of our dear brothers here departed, in the sure and certain hope' - I'm sorry, Mrs Mercer, I can't quite remember it all but you can be sure we said it properly at the time.

With our poor funeral ceremony over, the fit ones set off, half expecting to find the results of your husband's work the previous night and half expecting another Jap ambush. It was the former. Two Japs with their throats cut, three killed by single shots at close quarters and the last man, the one still holding his automatic weapon, with knife wounds which I cannot describe to you. Clearly the brave Private Mercer had despatched the entire patrol except one, who had had time to shoot before he too met his fate.

I don't know how far ahead he was looking, Mrs Mercer, whether he was trying to make life more likely for our wounded men or clearing the path homewards for the fit ones, or what. The result for the platoon was certainly a fine one. We all got back safely, including our wounded. I cannot tell you the debt we owe to Private Mercer. His was without question the bravest deed I ever saw or heard of in Burma and I have to tell you, from every man who knew him, that it was the greatest privilege to serve beside him.

Please do not try to reply to this letter here. I am meant to be shipped home shortly. I shall be in touch later. Yours most sincerely, A E Mycock, Lieutenant, 2nd Battalion York and Lancaster Regiment.

Mrs Mercer, Josephine, stared at the letter as if she expected it to do something - leap back into its envelope, perhaps, or play a tune. It was August 1944. She hadn't been to see the King yet but she knew she would be going shortly, with their only child, Michelle. It was Michelle's fifteenth birthday soon. There were almost enough coupons saved for the ingredients of a cake.

Josephine Mercer looked at her daughter, who had been listening to the letter being read out and whose face was contorted in the bitterest anger.

"Michelle, whatever is it? What's the matter, girl?"

"He didn't need to die, did he? It was his choice!" cried Michelle, her voice rising as she tried to control the sobs. "He went and died for them out there, when he should have saved himself for us. Victoria Cross! Who cares about a bloody Victoria Cross! Given by men, to men, for saving men. What use is that to us? And he did it on purpose. He forgot about us completely!"

"Michelle! Come back here! Michelle! And don't you dare swear like that in front of..."

Month by month, as the news of the war got better and better and the end seemed to be near, Michelle Mercer, quietly and secretly, grew more and more angry with her dead father. Not only had he given his life for the sake of a few Tommies, or Chindits or whatever they were called, but he'd done it when the war was almost over. It was like those soldiers in the previous war, shot at the front with only minutes to go to armistice. Except, of course, they didn't want to be shot and were not out looking for it. Her father had gone into the dark, dark jungle knowing there was a good chance that he was by his own actions making sure he'd never see his daughter again, or his wife. Michelle could not forgive him for his lack of care and duty.

Nor could she forgive her mother for accepting her man's death in that stupid, a-man's-got-to-do, outdated way. Just exactly why did a man have to do? Why did he have to leave his daughter and wife? What possible reason was there good enough for that?

As the new year turned of 1945, the war was almost finished and Michelle had come to understand her mother a little better. That stoical acceptance of Fate was included in the way they brought them up in the olden days. The women of her generation felt like that. They accepted their doom because that was how things were. You couldn't really blame her for it, although you might have thought she would be more receptive to Michelle's point of view.

The same understanding could not be extended to her late father. While mother saw it all as the hand of God, for King and Country, each of them moving in mysterious ways, Michelle saw it as a deliberate act of cruelty and irresponsibility. And then, to cap it all, mother started bringing another man into the house. This was an American, a navigator on a B-52 based in Lincolnshire who'd come to Buxton on a day out and met mother in the pub where she worked. He came over to stay on his next leave. Although he was supposed to be in the spare bedroom, Michelle knew he was in with mother. She heard them. She heard her mother giggling, and then trying to shush up the proceedings, and then moaning and crying out in passionate gratitude.

Michelle decided she hated the American. He had no business taking her father's place. Without knowing where she had the inspiration, she drew a picture of him in his fine American uniform and cut it out with scissors. She wrote his name on the back of the picture. She cut the picture in half, lengthways, and again widthways, saying as she did so, very slowly, 'May you navigate to Hell'. She lit the four pieces of paper in a saucer with a match and watched them flame and shrivel up, and then she doused them with spring water from St Anne's Well saying again, 'Navigate to Hell, navigate to Hell!'

Michelle was not surprised when the American failed to turn up at their house on his next leave. Nor was she altogether shocked when a telephone call to the airbase revealed that no information was available at this time, nor was she when another American came to the door to tell her mother that three B-52s had been lost over Germany in a daylight raid and her navigator was in one of the airplanes. Whether he had parachuted was not known. Next of kin had been informed.

The new American was a black man. Michelle had never seen a black man close to before, and neither had her mother. Apparently, the dead American had been one of the few on the base who was sympathetic to black people. Most of the others called him 'Boy' or 'Nigger' but the dead American was kind and reasonable. This was why he, the black man, had come to tell Michelle's mother, whom his friend had talked about and called by her name. Once he'd got to Buxton it hadn't been too hard to find her out.

Yes, he would stay for tea, but then he would have trains and buses to get him back to Gainsborough and then, if he was lucky, he might hop a ride back to base with someone out on the town. Otherwise he would have to walk the last five miles.

Over the next few weeks, Michelle watched in horrified fascination as her mother became the new American's lover. By May, when the war in Europe ended, they were planning their future together. There seemed a possibility that he might be posted to the Far East where Japan was still fighting, but it didn't happen and the two of them decided to go back to the USA together. Michelle would find that exciting, wouldn't she, a new life in the Land of the Free?

In the August, the Yanks bombed the Japs with a new kind of bomb and the Japs gave in. In Buxton, Josephine Mercer and her American looked forward to the peace, presumed that Miss M Mercer would fall in with their arrangements and made them accordingly, and failed to notice that Michelle was making a few arrangements of her own.

She was very nearly sixteen. She was not forced to go back to school. She walked up and down Spring Gardens looking at the shops. She thought she would like to work in a shop. Some of them didn't look like they would employ a girl of sixteen. The ironmonger's, for example, looked a very masculine sort of a place. Even the name, Shufflebotham, made it sound unsuitable for the genteel type of young lady Michelle was determined to become.

She didn't fancy the bank for the same reason, too masculine, and in any case it was a place where men built careers. They joined the bank and retired from the bank. That was not what Michelle had in mind.

The wine merchant thought she was joking when she asked about work, as if it were possible for a female, especially a very young female, to know anything about wine and spirits! It began to look like one of the grocery shops. The three main ones were the Maypole, The Home & Colonial Stores, and the International Stores.

The Maypole and the International didn't want anyone, thank you. The Home & Colonial was really looking for a boy to be apprenticed but boys were in short supply. A girl could do some of the work, well, most of it, really, and when they found a boy the girl could come upstairs to the shop and serve behind the counter.

So, Michelle would start the following week, in the cellars, weighing sugar and butter and lard into the tiny amounts allowed under rationing. If she did well enough at that, she could move on to tea and coffee.

Part two of Michelle's plan was to find somewhere to live. One room would do, preferably somewhere near Spring Gardens and the shop and, since her wages would only be a guinea a week, it would have to be cheap. She found the answer up on Silverlands, a top floor room in a big old house which at one time would have been rather grand with a wealthy family and servants filling every part. Now it was let to whoever wanted to be there for at least a week at a time. There was a choice of rates to pay. The higher included having the room cleaned and fresh sheets every week. Actors from the Opera House often stayed there on the lower rate, not the stars of course but the chorus girls and boys, some of the band maybe, and the bit-parters if it was a straight play.

If you were a longer term tenant, which Michelle certainly intended to be, you got even better terms. For five shillings a week you shared the laundry in the cellar, consisting of a wash boiler which you had to fuel yourself and a sink. You also shared the kitchen on the ground floor, which had a gas cooker on a penny meter, a kettle, a sink with cold running water and a table and chairs. Pots and pans were not provided nor indeed was anything else. If Michelle wanted to cook a meal, she would have to transport the ingredients and the utensils all the way down two flights of stairs, eat the result in the cold kitchen, wash up and take all back upstairs again. Coal had to be kept in sacks in the cellar, so that was three flights upstairs with the scuttle for the room fire, while trying to work out who was pinching your coal, and your kindling you kept in your room.

None of this frightened Michelle in the slightest. She was used to household chores. They were part of her life as they were part of every working-class girl's life. Michelle was excited by the idea of the independence and not at all disconcerted by the labour involved in keeping a life going or the likely lack of spare cash. This was but a means to an end, a step on the way, an investment in herself. Quite what the destination was, or the objectives, Michelle never bothered to identify. She was on the road to somewhere, that much she knew, and at this stage no details were necessary.

She had expected fuss from her mother. There was the ticket, bought and paid for, leaving from Liverpool on Monday, and here was the daughter saying she wasn't going. Mrs Mercer made little fuss because she knew there was no point in making any more. She knew Michelle. If Michelle said she wasn't going, the only way they would get her on that boat would be to knock her out, tie her up and put her in a trunk, which was not an option considering what would no doubt happen when she got out of it.

Mother said a modestly tearful farewell to her daughter. The American step-father-to-be shook her hand and Michelle waved goodbye as the train steamed out of Buxton station. That was that. She was on her own. She had a room, a job, a few friends from school, and two five-pound notes the American had slipped her during the handshake. She bought two penn'orth of chips and ate them as she walked home, to her new home, a room on top of an old house where, come October, the wind would find a way of blowing straight through the glass of the sash windows, and the rain would seep under the slates, down through the stone of the chimney and out through the plaster of the chimney breast.

Michelle fixed the wallpaper back to the wall with drawing pins since no paste would hold it against the wet. She had blazes as big as she could in that tiny grate, originally meant only as an occasional bedroom fire for a servant, a good reason for economy, but the windows steamed up and the damp seemed to get worse if anything. She wondered about a live-in job at one of the hotels. Such places, like the Palace Hotel, had radiators worked from a central boiler. A man was paid to shovel the coal into the boiler and everybody else had clean heat. That did sound attractive. The catch was the wages - very poor - and the hours - very long - and the treatment she could expect. At sixteen, all she would be offered was kitchen maid or chambermaid and a life filled with skivvying. She would stick with The Home and Colonial and her little coal fire, for the time being.

The Manager there, Mr Todder, liked to pop down to the cellar to make sure that Michelle was doing her work properly. He liked looking at Michelle from behind, as she stooped to fill her flour measure from the sack. Michelle was a tall, well built girl. She reminded Mr Todder of a statue he had once seen in a museum, except the statue had no arms and was bare to the waist. Michelle had a similar sort of face too, thought Mr Todder, a biggish, boldish kind of a face, with a proper chin and a high forehead, and a proper nose too. Quite noble, really, thought Mr Todder. Aristocratic. Her dark hair added to the impression because she wore it up, in a style which used to be popular when Mr Todder was an apprentice and the shop girls had waist-length hair which they pinned up like Michelle's. Nowadays they all had hair hardly to their shoulders and it was permed into waves all around, bangs he thought they were called, and a big wave on top at the front. He preferred the idea of Michelle's hair, long, falling to the waist when it was unpinned.

Mr Todder could not spend too long in the cellar, especially as Michelle did faultless work, nor could he go down there too often. He did like to go, though. He did like to go, always hoping that he might get into an ordinary kind of a conversation with the girl, but she remained resolutely respectful, speaking only when spoken to and then to the absolute minimum. Mr Todder assumed she was shy, so he tried a bit harder. She was embarrassed by his attentions. She went pink. Mr Todder retreated.

At Number 19, Robertson Road, one of the smaller houses in a nice, respectable area, Mrs Todder was what people used to call a scold. Whereas Mr Todder's word was law at The Home and Colonial Stores, it was not considered to be worth a farthing in the home and empire of Mrs Todder - given to the happy couple, as she never ceased to remind her spouse, by her very generous, wealthy and widely admired father.

Mr and Mrs Todder had never produced children, mostly because they very rarely had performed the necessary act - only enough, in the view of Mrs Todder, to consummate and cement the marriage. Mr Todder was very frustrated. He did have an occasional mistress, a widow from the Great War who had not remarried, considerably older than him but who enjoyed allowing him some comfort on the first Tuesday of the month. Otherwise his yearnings were realised only occasionally.

He recognised the dangers of being fanciful about Michelle. He was well aware that she was young, hardly sixteen, and that a wrong move on his part could bring disgrace. So, he was very circumspect but also conscious that an attractive girl like this could soon be walking out with a beau, a youthful and unmarried man, but probably also a lad with very little in the way of spending money. Here, he thought, was the way. He would offer her money - subtly, of course, and very, very softly-softly, but he felt sure that Michelle was a practical girl. He knew she was alone in the world, and he knew why. His moment would come, he was sure.

"Michelle" he said. "How do you find this work?"

"It's all right" said the girl.

"Don't you find it monotonous?"

"No, Mr Todder."

"Don't you find it hard, all this shifting sacks about and carrying things up to the shop?"

"No."

There was a pause, while Mr Todder collected his courage and Michelle poured sugar into rectangular bags made of thick, coarse, dark blue paper.

"Your wages" said Mr Todder.

Michelle said nothing.

"You realise I can't do anything about them as such. In point of fact, the wage for this job is set by the people at head office. At the head office of The Home and Colonial Stores Limited. I only have a very limited amount of flexibility as regards wages, and I have already exercised this flexibility in your favour as much as possible."

"Very kind I'm sure, Mr Todder, very kind" said Michelle which, if you took the average of conversations between her and Mr Todder, was a long speech and encouraging to the ardent manager.

"When I say I can't do anything about it, I mean to say, in point of fact, that is only insofar as the shop is concerned. Given the circumstances in this connection, there are other possibilities to be investigated, if you might be interested. Out of hours, in point of fact."

"What, evening work, you mean?" Somehow, Michelle felt she was in charge of this, whatever it was.

"Well, yes, kind of evening work, you could say. Of a personal nature, in point of fact. Not to do with sugar and tea, as it were."

"To do with what, then, Mr Todder?"

"I'm a generous man, Michelle. I have earned my position in life with hard work and I can openly admit that the financial rewards are more than acceptable. I have money and I am able to give it, in return for services rendered, in a manner of speaking."

"Services?"

"Yes, quite, Miss Mercer, you see, beneath this exterior of grim authority and grocery expertise beats the heart, in point of fact, of an artist. I work with the camera, mainly, but I also draw and paint. I have my own studio, very private, and I mean to say that, should you be willing to think in terms of, er, as it might be, having a mind to present yourself pleasantly and graciously, perhaps as it might be in your partial deshabilles, not necessarily entirely as nature intended if such might in any way distress...er, I could offer you a handsome fee. No touching of course, simply to view, as such, the female form as art and for artistic purposes only, ah...?"

"Pose? How much?"

Mr Todder could hardly contain himself. He knew that this could be the beginning of an entirely new parallel life in paradise. He must not offer her too much, or she would infer that there was more to the deal than was ostensibly intended. Nor must he offer her too little. He must not imply that he thought her services anything other than of the first order. Her worth demanded payment of the top rank.

"I was thinking, perhaps, fifteen shillings. An hour, that is. Fifteen shillings an hour."

"A pound."

"Oh, er, yes, very well. A pound it is. Perhaps we could start tomorrow? If you could meet me after the shop closes, at the Silverlands end of Holker Road?"

"You're not expecting to do it in my room, are you?"

"No, no Miss Mercer. My studio is just near there. Very discreet, I assure you."

"What should I bring to wear?"

"You don't need to bring anything, Miss Mercer."

"What? You said not entirely as nature. I'm not doing entirely for a quid an hour. Entirely will cost you more than that. A lot more."

Mr Todder could hardly speak. He was in a complete triumphal panic.

"I simply meant, Miss Mercer, that I shall provide everything you need. Some classical style robes, some diaphanous drapes, that sort of thing. You will have seen classical paintings where, ah, how shall we put it, certain parts of the female form are visible, purely for artistic reasons in point of fact, and certain parts remain covered."

"You want to see my tits, you mean."

"Miss Mercer, please! We can go into this at the time. If we assume that the first session will be two hours, here are two pound notes. Now, if you will excuse me..."

Michelle had a little smile to herself as she tucked the money into her knickers and went back to weighing up the tea. In one hour she could earn very nearly what she got for a week in The Home and Colonial. And what was wrong with showing the old man what she'd been given by the gods of femininity? Perhaps there were other men who would be willing to pay. She could have every day off! If she only worked two evenings a week she'd be pulling more than a skilled man with a family to support. If she worked three evenings...

Mr Todder's studio was at the back of a house, converted into flats and bedsits, which sat neatly between two street lights. On a dark night like this they walked into the shadows, turned into the drive and were through the private door to the studio in moments. No-one, unless they were spying, could have seen them.

Inside the studio was paraphernalia familiar to any experienced model but new to Miss Mercer. White sheets on frames and white umbrellas for reflecting light, curtains, tripods, cameras and several painted backdrops. There was a small table set with cutlery and glass, anticipating a photographic dinner for two. Michelle was more concerned to find a changing room and was pleased to see a fairly substantial cubicle in the corner rather than the curtained-off sort of thing you got in the department stores.

Mr Todder was trying hard to contain his excitement but his intended impression of the cool professional was not altogether convincing. Michelle was beginning to have doubts. Mr Todder was no muscleman but he was bigger than she was and certainly stronger.

"I'd like you to start by wearing this" he said, showing her a pale green gown made of several layers of muslin. It was classical Empire line, with a ribbon tied under the bodice and not a very low neck although the dress was low at the back. Quite modest, really, thought Michelle, her doubts easing slightly. She went into the cubicle, was happy to see that it could be locked, did lock it and changed into the dress. It was loose fitting and swirly. She felt kind of free in it, as if she wanted to run barefoot through the long grass. Looking in the mirror she realised that she could not wear her brassiere with it because the straps showed at the back and there was a further hint of Messrs Berlei revealed at the neckline.

She took the brassiere off and wondered about her slip. It was just a waist length one. You couldn't see it but all the same she felt as if it detracted from the effect. She took it off, for a moment playfully considering removing her knickers too but immediately deciding against.

Michelle stepped from the cubicle like a dancer coming on stage in Swan Lake. Mr Todder was mesmerised as he looked up from fiddling with his camera. His hands trembled so much that he almost knocked the tripod and all to the floor.

"Miss Mercer!" he cried. "What a picture you are!"

She was posed first against the white sheets and then against a backdrop of trees and flowers. She was turned this way and that, arms placed so, head at such an angle, could she just place her foot on this stool. Mr Todder moved some of his lights around. Michelle didn't realise but she was now back-lit and her figure was outlined inside the dress. Mr Todder was beside himself at the shadowy silhouette of such perfection. He had initially resolved to keep it to modest dresses for at least the first two or three sessions, but really the show so far was proving too much for his moral fibre.

"Miss Mercer. I wonder if you could now change into this? It is meant to imitate that picture, you know, of the French revolution, where the brave heroine carries the flag forward against the enemy."

"With one breast showing" replied Michelle, her tone having the same effect on Todder's flow of flimflam as alum has on a bleeding cut. "Right. Won't be a moment."

This was it. This was the test, brought forward possibly in too much haste but not looking like it as she strode to the cubicle. Mr Todder wondered if he would regret not being more patient. His long-term aim was to have Michelle naked with her hair down, her long dark hair concealing and revealing as she struck various poses and his camera flashed. That was long term. By then, they would be on much more intimate social terms too. He might show her how to work the camera. She might like to take pictures of him, naked. But that was long term. Of course, there was no telling how long 'long' would be.

In the changing room, Michelle was looking at herself in the mirror. She certainly had a splendid body. If the gods had given her this, surely she was meant to be proud of it and to make the most of it. She pulled the material back a little, to expose more of her left breast. Poor old Mr Todder. He'd have a heart attack. She wrapped her woollen cardigan around her as a shawl and went out into the studio.

"Where do you want me to be?" she asked.

"I'm sure you don't need any backdrop, Miss Mercer. Stand by the white screen. You will be sufficient unto yourself. Consider the lilies of the field, how they grow. They toil not, neither do they spin, yet Solomon in all his glory...oh!"

It was impossible to suppress the gasp as Michelle took off her cardigan, threw it aside and stood like a flamenco dancer, hand on hip, head tossed back. Todder thought he had never seen anything so superb. Her bosom was like marble, it was like that statue he had seen.

Staring through the viewfinder was even more exciting. Here she was, framed and lit exclusively for him, with no distractions. She was a goddess. She was a miracle. His goddess. His miracle. There for him alone.

The camera crashed to the floor as Todder made his rush. He was on her before she could recover from the shock and the noise. His hands ripped the dress apart and grabbed at her breasts. His mouth slavered as he tried to kiss her neck and then opened in a soundless scream as a fish fork, secretly taken as a weapon from the set table and kept hidden in her hand just in case, stabbed fiercely into his private parts.

He staggered back. The fork dangled from the crotch of his trousers and blood ran along its handle.

"Miss Mercer! What have you done? You have killed me!"

Michelle was entranced by what she saw. The blood flowed down the handle and dripped onto the floor as Todder stood there, legs apart, his face a picture of terror, his hands waving aimlessly as his brain failed to decide whether or not to pull out the fork. For a moment Michelle was tempted to grab the fork and shove it in further. Instead she stepped into the cubicle, changed rapidly into her day clothes and left without a word, watched by a motionless, stupified, three-tined Todder.

CHAPTER TWO

"MICHELLE? Can I speak to you for a moment?"

Michelle turned, wiping the flour from her hands onto her apron, to find Mrs Chapman who was one of the senior serving ladies.

"Hello, Mrs Chapman? Don't usually see you down here." Mrs Chapman, Michelle thought, considered herself a little above the other staff and certainly the superior of any cellar-bound flour-bag filler.

"No, well, it's perhaps because I've already spent more than enough of my life doing your job. You didn't know that, did you? Thought I was always 'Yes, Mrs Chapman, no, Mrs Chapman'? I was just like you, except older. I had to start where you are, only I was 22, 1940, one of the first war widows in Buxton. Desperate I was. I worked here, underground, for a year or more, crying my tears into the sugar and flour until..."

"Until what, Mrs Chapman?"

"Until I did what you did. Posed. For him."

Michelle was unable to speak for a moment. Mrs Chapman was a handsome woman but surely too dignified, too conventional for the type who takes her clothes off in front of a stranger.

"I know what you're thinking, Michelle. Too respectable to strip off? Well, I have a good figure. A lot better than Mrs Todder's. And I didn't mind doing it. The money was good and very welcome, after my Donald was killed in the war. Then Todder spoiled it, as I guess he did with you. The difference was, I had a year of posing before he had a go at me. He must have found you much more tempting."

"How do you know all this, Mrs Chapman? About that night, if I might ask?"

"That's why I've come to see you. Ever since my equivalent of that night, two years ago now, Todder has been giving me seven and six a week to keep quiet. I've got used to that money. It's part of my economy, you might say. A significant part. Goodness knows, we don't get much off The Home and Colonial. Now Todder says he can't pay me any more. He says he's destroyed all the plates from our sessions and I can't prove anything. But if I keep quiet I can keep my job. So, I put two and two together. You're new, you're good looking, you're well upholstered. I will bet anything you like that you've been to Todder's studio, he's had a go, and you've asked him for money. Too much money. Is that right, or not?"

"He had a go, as you put it, on the first night. I was in my second costume."

"That would be the heroine from the French revolution."

"That was her."

"So you never got as far as the water nymph in the pool?"

"Water nymph? I'd only joined the revolution for two minutes before he came at me like a mad octopus."

"Oh, Michelle, you haven't lived. He's got this amazing kind of wire ring thing, adjustable for height, with a sort of parchment skin covering the ring. It's got water lillies painted on it. Well, there's a hole in the middle, and you stand there in the hole with the ring of parchment around your waist, and if that's all you can see it looks a bit like you're standing up to your waist in water. Which it does, in the photographs. Sort of. But the main feature of the photographs is not the water."

"You mean you have your bosom exposed. All of it."

"That's it. He showed me this painting. Pre-Raphaelite, whatever that means. There were about a dozen of these nymphs standing in the water with nothing on. He said I was to pose in the grand tradition of the great artists of the past. Well, I suppose they used to grope their models just like Todder. He may not be a great artist but he's just the same in every other respect."

"Mrs Chapman. What about the seven and six?"

"Yes. He said he couldn't afford it any longer, as circumstances had changed. 'Something unforeseen has occurred' he said, 'in point of fact, to affect adversely my pecuniary capabilities'. Pompous idiot. Why can't he say he's broke, instead of all this lah-di-dah double mouthful. So I assume you've asked the dirty old sod for a good whack. A sovereign a week? More? Thirty bob?"

"I asked him for two. Two pounds a week. I said how it would look in the paper, how he would be seen as my guardian while my mum was in America, and how he'd abused his trust with an innocent young girl."

"Very good, Michelle, very good. Heart-strings are for plucking. Only problem is, whatever his airs and graces and whatever he might tell you, he's just about skinned already, without your two quid. There's three of us in this shop getting seven and six, plus he pays good rates to the professional models he hires. No hanky-panky with them, mind, but they do strip off entirely. So, if he gives you two quid, that means he has to stop everything else. In fact, I don't know how he's kept going as long as he has. The money coming in can't be all that brilliant. A grocer's shop manager, I mean. And there's Mrs Todder, and Todder Towers to keep up. Can't be cheap, all that."

"What do you want me to do about it? You've all been getting your three half crowns for years. I've not had a single instalment yet."

"Reduce your price. Make it seven and six like the rest of us."

"Not on your nellie. I'm having two quid. He would have raped me if I hadn't..."

"Hadn't what?"

"I stabbed him. In the pills. With a fish fork."

"Michelle, you might have killed him!"

"No, not really. Superficial wound. More by luck than good management, I have to admit - that it was superficial, I mean."

"I thought he was walking funny. You know, when he goes to the door to let Mrs So-and-so out and wish her good day. I think there were three whole days when he never went to the door at all!"

The two women dissolved in laughter and were still giggling when Miss Eddowes, the cashier, came down the stairs. Her normally po face was under strain. Miss Eddowes' face was legendary for its lack of movement. It showed no favours to anyone and it showed no prejudice either. In her capacity, in charge of the till and all monies, her face bestowed the same neutrality on each customer, whether it was 'That will be threepence farthing this morning, Mrs Brown' or 'That will be one pound, thirteen shillings and sevenpence, Mrs Green'. No, you could not accuse Miss Eddowes of taking sides or betraying her emotions, if she had any. But now her face was slightly askew. Michelle and Mrs Chapman might have said that Miss Eddowes was feeling a Capstan Full Strength emotion for the first time in her almost forty years.

"I don't think there's very much to laugh about" she said. "You had better come upstairs, both of you."

The staff were all assembled and the shop door was shut and locked. PC Nicholson, one of the local bobbies and a very, very large specimen of his breed, was standing there half-filling the shop on his own and looking uncomfortable as the only man among so many females.

"Ladies" he said. "Ladies. I have some very bad news for you. I won't beat about the bush. This morning, Mr Todder was found dead."

All the women except Michelle and Miss Eddowes gasped, let out a little cry, put their hands to their mouths or otherwise showed their shock. PC Nicholson continued.

"I can tell you what happened, because it will be all around town anyway. Mr Todder had his head in the gas oven. It was only by sheer good fortune that the house didn't explode when Mrs Todder switched the kitchen light on. One of you, quickly, get a glass of water!"

Miss Eddowes, the immovable Miss Eddowes, had fainted quite away.

The funeral was at the enormous St James' Church in Bath Road where Mr and Mrs Todder had attended every Sunday since they were married, holidays and sickness permitting. The funeral service strongly implied that the late Mr Todder was now nearer to God, which was the reward awaiting the repentant sinner and regular church-goer, and one day the estimable and virtuous Mrs Todder would join him for eternity in the heavenly chorus.

Such a forecast would have given the living Mr Todder serious cause for thought. It would have pulled him up sharply and made the gas oven much less attractive. Mr Todder had often wondered if Mrs Todder was God's vengeance upon him for his dark photographic secrets and even darker thoughts. He had hoped, as he drifted away in his own little cloud of town gas, that God would forgive him all his sins, including the one he was committing at that moment. He knew that if ever Mrs Todder found out about his photographs there would be no forgiveness from that quarter and she would probably be able to turn God against him too. His last acts therefore had been to destroy all his pictures and plates, give away his cameras and dismantle his studio props. He paid his rent up to the end of the next half year. Discretion by the studio landlord could be relied on and so earthly matters were settled. There was no mortgage on the house, there would be a pension from The Home and Colonial and Mrs Todder had some money from her late father.

She would be all right, and she wouldn't miss her husband in the slightest except as a useful and convenient whipping boy.

And so it had come to pass that, at peace with the world and in the hope of redemption, Mr Todder had taken a tasselled and embroidered cushion from the sofa and placed it on the bottom of the oven which, under Mrs Todder's cleansing and purification regimen, even though they had had no domestic help since 1940, was as clean now as it had been when the cooker was bought fifteen years before. He turned the oven control to Regulo 6 and lay down on the floor, also perfectly clean, with his head upon the cushion. He smiled as the plain sibilance of the gas ushered in the sacred gold and silver notes of harps and angels.

Mrs Todder didn't seem disposed to ask the staff of The Home and Colonial Stores back to her house for the funeral tea. The women had anticipated this and arranged their own tea at The Cheshire Cheese pub on the High Street. There had been some arguments put forward in favour of Miller's Cafe but it was felt on balance that licensed premises would be more appropriate.

They were all there, the full-timers, the part-timers, the Saturday girl, everybody. Some had halves of beer, a couple had stout, one asked for wine but of course there wasn't any so she had a glass of cider, another had a port and lemon, and Miss Eddowes had a sweet sherry. Miss Eddowes, as the senior person present, bought the first round - much to everyone else's astonishment, especially when they realised it had cost five shillings and eightpence, and even more so when she insisted after that on getting another round. Miss Eddowes' sherry didn't seem to last quite as long as the other drinks so she got herself a flyer, and another, and by the time the ham salad was served she was on her fifth. Five small sherries is not exactly a formidable, Bacchanalian, orgiastic amount of liquor but it was enough for Miss Eddowes. While they were all helping themselves at the buffet table she began to tell a rather sad story.

It emerged in small pieces, this story, couched in euphemism and encrypted by a sherry-induced slur, but of the listening girls four had no trouble at all in recognising the gist of it. The others there might have been too plain looking and so unqualified to have been approached about photographic modelling by the deceased - unlike, it transpired, Miss Eddowes! Miss

Eddowes, some years ago, had been quite a beauty. She had never, she admitted in a roundabout way, been Junoesque in stature but she had had a good face and a fine rather than pronounced figure. Mr Todder had liked it anyway. Mr Todder had seen it, all of it, many times. Mr Todder had...

Through the tears and the sobs, Michelle and Mrs Chapman gathered that where Todder had failed with them, he had succeeded with Miss Eddowes. Todder had allowed Miss Eddowes to think that he had the courage to leave his wife for her, and so she had allowed him to have his evil way. There had not been a baby, thank goodness, although she had wished for one at the time.

Gradually it had become clear to Miss Eddowes that the cowardly, deceitful Todder would never do anything more than take advantage of her, so she withdrew his privileges having first made sure that her promotion to cashier was immediate and permanent. Ever since then she had been with no man, nor did she ever want to. And now, she thought, she had better go home.

It being a private party and out of normal opening hours, there were no other customers in the Cheese to witness this extraordinary confession. While Miss Eddowes stood at the door, swaying slightly as she waited for the landlady to unlock and let her out, the rest of the guests sat in silence. Those who had not been members of the Todder Photographic Society had not understood the modelling part of the story but they had certainly got the full implications of the rest. Miss Eddowes! Doing it with Mr Todder!

Ham, lettuce, tomato, hard boiled egg, cucumber, pickled beetroot, spring onions, salad cream and bread and best butter were politely and thoughtfully consumed without a word, every pair of eyes staring ahead, vainly trying to imagine the scene.

Mrs Chapman was the first to crack. Her third port and lemon was doing its work and she giggled. One of the non-members, a married woman with four children at school and a war-wounded husband at home, giggled. Michelle giggled. Someone protested, eyes watering and cough racking, that a bit of hard boiled egg had gone down the wrong way. The landlady, who had heard everything, brought out a tray with another round of drinks, on the house with her own G&T in place of the late lamented sweet sherry. Her tears of laughter fell in the drinks. The place resounded with female ribaldry.

Whenever the peals started to quieten, one of the group would say half a sentence and they'd all ring out again at full volume.

"I bet they did it in the shop behind the counter..."
"...standing up against the bacon..."
"...with her back against the broken bisc..."
"That will be two and eleven this morning, Mr T..."
"Have you nothing smaller, Mr T..."
"I'll have a quarter of your Continental sausage..."

And so it was that, in laughter and merriment, the unamusing Mr Todder, photographer and grocer, moved from the present to the past, regretted hardly at all by any except poor Miss Eddowes, herself a somewhat regrettable case.

The new manager at The Home and Colonial Stores had very bad dandruff and smelled unpleasantly. He had a fat belly against which rubbed a shirt which wasn't quite as clean as it might have been. As well as the dandruff, further unattractive aspects of his head included little flecks of surplus Brylcreem on his bald patch, blackheads on his cheeks and bad breath.

Michelle waited a day or two to see if things became any better but they did not and so she went to see the owners of Miller's Cafe in Spring Gardens, who recruited her willingly as a waitress. The basic wage wasn't quite as good as Mr Todder's top-of-the-range flour-packing money had been, but tips would make it equal or more. Besides, she could see people, talk to them, be part of a scene which constantly changed rather than staring alone and forever into a blue sugar bag.

Young men used to come in the middle of the day, the smarter type of young men, the ones who worked in the banks and the lawyers' offices and the clerical departments of businesses. These young men went out to lunch once or even twice a week, some of them more often than they should once they had been served by Miss Mercer, who looked very fetching indeed in her black dress and white pinafore, with her dark hair up and perched upon it a starched little hat.

Occasionally, a young man would fetch up his courage and ask Michelle if she would like to walk out with him, perhaps to the Spa Cinema where there was a John Wayne on this week, or an Anna Neagle, with Greta Gynt in the second feature. Automatically, Michelle refused the first few but then began to think, why not? Why should I go home every night to my room with nothing but the wireless and the gas meter for company?

She said yes one day to a good looking young man from Martin's Bank. He was tall with a clearly defined nose and chin but he was fairly boring, one of those who liked to tell in great detail what had happened that day with the cash ledger. Both films were good, a Ronald Reagan western and an English tear-jerker set in a railway station. The young man bought her an ice cream, they held hands and he tried to kiss her but didn't seem to mind too much when she dodged him. She tried to discuss the film as he walked her home. She explained that she thought Trevor Howard a very dashing and handsome man but she admitted she couldn't get away with Celia Johnson's accent. They didn't talk like that in Buxton, did they? Not even the poshest woman she knew, the wife of the owner of the bookshop, talked like that. The young man was slightly bemused by this kind of conversation. It was based on opinions, not facts, and he found that difficult. He didn't really have opinions himself and couldn't quite understand how they were arrived at.

He and Michelle went out again to the pictures. It was a poor bill, with a Tex Ritter western and a George Raft gangster film. Even the newsreel was dull. He tried to kiss her again, and she let him, sort of. He found it about as exciting as kissing the spine of a book and tried to liven things up by putting his hand on her knee. She took his hand away. He tried again. She took his hand away. He tried again. She took his hand firmly in hers, raised his fingers to her lips as if to kiss them, and bit them very hard instead.

A few people in the rows in front turned around at the strangled yelp and those on either side looked in the flickering shadows to see what caused it. They only saw an impassive and very pretty girl watching the film intently while her young man appeared to be so moved by the death of George Raft's moll that he had tears in his eyes and was wringing his hands in grief.

Michelle's next romantic assignment was with a quite different sort, a rakish kind of a lad with money. She could tell he had money because he left large tips under his saucer, sometimes a sixpence and once even a shilling, and through the cafe window she could see his car parked on the street, a red MG TC. He generally wore a tweed suit. With his Kangol cap and yellow scarf, and the leather gloves he had for driving, the impression was of a young country gentleman who very much enjoyed living on the proceeds of work done by others.

This was a true enough impression, apart from the country part. In fact, his father owned a quarry rather than a farming estate but the result for the son was much the same. Young Gerald didn't like quarrying, no more than he would have liked farming or any other kind of serious endeavour. His mother thought him a wonder of the century and far too noble to get involved with a lot of dirty limestone, explosives, shovels, picks and even dirtier workmen. Gerald's mother encouraged him to play the part of gentry while ensuring that her husband, by long and deep involvement with a lot of dirty limestone, explosives and shovels, kept up the flow of £.s.d. necessary to her own and her fine son's requirements.

Most of the girls Gerald met were Pony Club, tennis club, golf club, rugby club girls. Some of them thought him an upstart and cut him. Some thought him a waster and couldn't be bothered with him. Some thought him a bit of a pirate, an adventurer and therefore an adventure to be with. He played centre three-quarter back for the Buxton 1st XV where he was unknown for his tackling prowess but much admired for his ability to dance, dodge, dummy and sway his way past the opposition, often as far as the try line. On balance, it was felt, he brought the team more points with his attacking flair than he lost with his unwillingness to fight in the last ditch, and so he always had his place.

Of course, the girls who came to the rugby club were more disposed towards the looks and talents of a try-scoring dancing centre than those of a grunting hooker or sweating, gorilla-like flanker. The more disposed they were, the more willing they proved to caress and be caressed. A number of triumphant episodes with such girls led Gerald to believe that he was God's most compassionate and considerate gift to the female sex. After a run of effortless successes, he took it for granted that a member of said sex lucky enough to be selected by him would deny him nothing in a bed, a dappled glade, a haystack, standing up against a wall behind the cycle sheds or wherever they happened to be having a fumble.

Michelle was not a rugby club girl. She was not a member of the Pony Club nor had the thought of joining the tennis club yet crossed her mind. Michelle was a waitress in a cafe, a member of the working class, possibly, as far as Gerald knew, the daughter of one of his father's awful quarrymen. After several occasions of tea and toasted teacake, such considerations were obliterated by Michelle's bosom as she served him, Michelle's rear as she walked away from him, and Michelle's beautious features when she smiled at him through the cafe window as he posed for a moment beside the MG, surruptitiously looking to see if she had picked up his tip.

One day, he asked her if she would like to go for a drive on her afternoon off. She would, so Gerald said he would pack a picnic. If the weather turned out badly, they would keep the hood up and eat their picnic in the car. Unfortunately - as it turned out - the sun shone and the birds sang. Gerald drove to a quiet spot somewhere in the hinterland beyond Longnor and Crowdecote, where there was a small piece of woodland and a view to the valley of the River Dove below. He spread a fine cloth on the grass and brought forth an even finer picnic. He hoped Miss Mercer, may I call you Michelle, liked wine. Had she ever had wine before? This was real French wine, naturally, and Michelle was certain to enjoy it. She should sip it rather than take it like the beer which she, perhaps, was more used to.

Gerald was very pleased at the way Michelle enjoyed her wine. She had finished her third glass before they got to the apple pie and was quite giggly. After the apple pie she lay back, replete and happy, and this was where the hero always leaned over the heroine and planted the first kiss. She would then throw her arms around him and Bob would be his uncle.

The wine had indeed made Michelle more relaxed than usual. She quite enjoyed his kiss, well, almost enjoyed, but felt all the old fears and panics rush back the second he touched her. She could not bear to be touched. He put his hand on her breast and that was that. Blindly reaching for the nearest object, she missed the cutlery but found a bone from a turkey leg and stabbed him in the temple with it. He rolled away, stood, and reeled back a few steps, feeling his head with his hand then looking at it, expecting to see rivers of blood transferred from his gaping wound.

He cursed her for a stupid, priggish little waitress who didn't realise how grateful she should be. She should have known what was expected of her when she agreed to come out with him. Good heavens! French wine, turkey, everything the best. She should be pulling her knickers down and asking for it, not stabbing him with an offensive bone!

Michelle stood up, thought for a moment about laying him out with the wine bottle, and set off in a homewards direction. She could walk to Longnor, it wasn't far, only a couple of miles, and there'd be a bus from there. Gerald could clear up the picnic.

"Thank you for a lovely afternoon" she said, smiling sweetly. "I'm sorry I didn't realise what was expected of me and that I am only a stupid waitress. I do hope you find someone locally who meets your specification. Goodbye."

There were several other very brief encounters with similar endings and Michelle came to realise that she was not quite normal in this. She talked to the other waitresses, or rather they told her about various goings on, which made it quite clear that while boys were only after one thing, girls were often happy to conspire to agree in theory. The chase and the catch made a game in which neither party was ever quite sure if they were the predator or the prey. Sometimes, at the kill, even if she had been the chaser, the girl would surrender. She would comply with what the boy wanted, partly or totally.

Michelle could not share these girls' enthusiasm for boys as a species nor understand the importance and status attached to the boy-girl game, but she could see that it was the done thing and that she wasn't doing it. Clearly, she was the odd one out, there was something wrong with her. Good Lord, even old Miss Eddowes had had a go.

Michelle resolved to give boys another try. The next time an agreeable young man asked her out, she would say yes, and she would permit him to...well, permit him to do something, at any rate. Once she got over the first wave of panic, she would be all right.

CHAPTER THREE

THE young man designated by the Fates to fulfil the role of seducer, or at least introducer, was one Ernest Mycock, a studious, serious but also amusing kind of a chap who was working as a junior clerk with a firm of surveyors. One day he would be Ernest Mycock ARICS, a professional man, a member of Rotary, a mason, perhaps even a representative of the people on Buxton Urban District Council. The young Ernest performed his duties with diligence and accuracy but his heart and soul were somewhere else entirely. Ernest Mycock was actually going to be a writer. He was a great admirer of Arnold Bennett and J B Priestley and, in his more reckless moments, Ernest admitted to a strong liking for D H Lawrence. Possibly Ernest would become the D H Lawrence of Buxton, perhaps with elements of Bennett and Priestley incorporated. Possibly he would become the Ernest Mycock of Buxton, with nobody else's elements. Meanwhile, he read books like other people drank tea, ate meals, put on their hats and coats. The staff of the library wondered why he kept coming back for surely he must have read every book in the place twice over.

His writing was very secret. He was working on several books at the moment, both fiction and non-fiction, and he would tell Michelle all about them one day. He had told Michelle the rest of it, about his ambitions and the authors he admired, on the train to Ashbourne, and on the train to Chesterfield, and on the train to Manchester.

Very rapidly they established a pattern for their days out. Michelle and Ernest clicked and, just for once, Michelle was happy to be led, organised and given no choices. She could trust Ernest. It was transparently obvious that she could trust him. So Ernest did the organising. He would discover that there was a cultural event of some kind somewhere, and they would take the train to it. Also, as their relationship developed, one night a week they went to the pictures, and on Sundays they went to church followed by Sunday dinner cooked by Mrs Mycock, mother of Ernest and, like so many, a war widow. Sunday dinner was always a spectacular event. Mrs Mycock had a marvellously fruitful and well worked allotment to account for the vegetables - and the eggs, because she ran a few Rhode Island Reds on it too - but she must have had superb contacts to account for the rest. Today it was a shoulder of mutton got from a farmer they knew in Monyash, with peas, roast potatoes, cabbage and broad beans, preceded by Yorkshire pudding with onion gravy and succeeded by a Bakewell pudding. The Bakewell must have used up the family's butter and sugar rations for a month all by itself, and where did she get ground almonds?

It was after one of these midday extravaganzas, when Michelle and Ernest were flopped on the parlour settee while mother washed up, that the girl suddenly realised.

"Ernest Mycock? Ernest Mycock! Any relation to Lieutenant Mycock, A E, 2nd Battalion York and Lancaster?"

"He was my father."

"Was?"

"Yes, he was killed in the war."

"No he wasn't! He lived! It was my father who was killed, not yours! We had a letter! He lived, your father! He...lived" she ended limply and lamely, noticing the disappointment and hurt on Ernest's face. "I'm sorry, Ernest. You see, my father was with your father in the jungle. We had a letter. From him. After dad was..."

"I see. Well, all I can tell you is that their patrol was attacked. They left the wounded behind, like they always did, and my father was one of them. Even though he was the platoon's officer, they still left him. Anyway, because one particularly brave fellow had been out on his own and slit all the Nips' throats, the coast was clear for them to get back. Except my father was so badly wounded that he died a month later in the hospital at Rangoon."

"Your dad wrote a letter to my mum. He wrote it from the hospital, but he said..."

"What?"

"He said he was coming home to England. He didn't say he was going to die. I'm sorry, Ernest."

"Haven't you got a hanky? Here, use this. Look, stop it, will you? You're making me cry now."

"Sorry. There. I won't cry any more. And he didn't say, either, that he was one of the wounded left behind. In the letter, I mean."

"This letter made a big impression."

"So it should. I read it a thousand times if I read it once. You see, I was very angry with my dad. He was killed. There was no need for it. He left me and mum alone in the world, for the sake of..."

"So he was the one. Of course, Mercer VC! How stupid of me. He was the brave fellow who went out. He died to save my father and the other soldiers. And you would rather..."

"And I would rather he hadn't! Yes! That's right! I would rather he was still here. And if you don't understand that, you don't understand anything!"

Ernest put his arm around Michelle and she wept into his jumper. Gradually her sobbing stopped and her breathing evened out. They were both asleep when mum looked in so she crept out again, made herself a cup of tea, and sat at the kitchen table thinking, as she so often did, of Lieutenant Albert Ernest Mycock, 2nd Battalion York and Lancaster Regiment, the engineering student from Sheffield University she had married in 1928, partly because she was pregnant with Ernest junior but mostly because she was utterly in love with him. She went to live with his parents while Ernest finished his studies. She saw him at week-ends for almost two years, and then he went to work for months at a time in one colony or another while she still lived with the in-laws. After ten years of marriage he finally got a job which kept him at home and they bought a nice house in Burbage. One year later, Germany invaded Poland.

Being 29 and a mining engineer, Albert Ernest Mycock could probably have seen the war out without getting too involved but he had to volunteer, and he would pick a regiment which one day would be assigned to the mad, bad and dangerous to know Orde Wingate, the General who invented the Chindits and thought what a good idea it would be to get behind the Japanese lines in Burma and cause a lot of bother. And the consequence was, Lieutenant Mycock ended up dead in Rangoon. Well, at least she had her son. He was a steady sort, and this Michelle seemed nice.

Mrs Mycock's reveries were cut short by a rumpus elsewhere in the house. She went into the corridor in time to see Michelle disappearing out of the front door in tears and her son standing there looking hopeless and helpless.

"What happened, son? Where's Michelle going?"

"I'm sorry, mum. I don't actually know. I don't actually know what happened."

Two long days went by and Ernest didn't come to the cafe. When he did, it was as if there had been no incident between them except that, yes, there was a slight coolness. There had to be. They both pretended that things were the same, but things were not the same. They resumed their routine - outing, pictures, church, lunch, outing, pictures, church, lunch.

There was no hanky panky. There never had been, but there had always been the distinct if distant possibility. Now, Ernest and Michelle most definitely were just good friends. Ernest, being Ernest, didn't seem to mind this but Michelle, who actively wanted something to happen, could see pale friendship developing into stalemate. After three weeks, she decided she would do something about it. She consulted her workmates and the next afternoon found her in a field, staring nervously at a gypsy caravan while a short, stout, brown and white horse gave her one uninterested half glance before getting back to the business of the day, which consisted mostly of slow and gentle chomping of the excellent local fare.

The caravan, Michelle might have been interested to know, was of the Reading type, built in 1919 by Messrs Dunton, in Reading, and restored during the war years to its full glory by an old woodcarver and painter down New Forest way. When people came along and saw it in his yard and asked to buy it, the old man said no, it wasn't for sale. He was quite sure about that. But when an olive-skinned gypsy beauty with long black hair and skirts that swept the floor came a-knocking, the old man wasn't so firm in his refusal. Three days later the caravan was making its way north, pulled by the said brown and white horse whose sturdiness, massive quarters and intelligent application proved its fell-pony ancestry.

The gypsy woman hadn't particularly meant to find Buxton, much less to stay there for any length of time. It was uphill, steeply uphill, whichever way you came to it and hardly a suitable destination for a horse, no matter how willing and able, pulling a gypsy living waggon weighing rather more than a ton. Still, they somehow arrived there and the driver thought the horse deserved a good rest. The farmer with fields on the south side of Buxton was quite happy for her to stay for a modest rent. He was a farmer of the old school, a man tolerant of travelling folk, a man who used to farm with horses and appreciated the skills gypsies had with them. It might have been a different story. He doubtless would not have been so agreeable if she had been one of your modern tinkers, with a motor van pulling a plain wagon with a canvas bow-top. That was not the same at all. All that type of tinker wanted to do was buy your scrap metal for nothing and steal anything he could lift. No, but your proper gypsy, the kind you used to get, now he was a different character altogether.

The gypsy woman agreed heartily with the farmer on all these points, forecast a long and happy life for each one of the farmer's children and their children too, and began making a modest but sufficient living out of fortune telling. Most of her clients were female, and mostly they were young, and here was another one standing outside, wavering, wondering, hesitating.

What a beautiful thing the caravan was, Michelle thought to herself. The main body of it was red, a dark kind of red which she thought was in her old paintbox and called Crimson Lake. There were painted carvings in a much brighter red with green and gold. The wheels and pieces underneath were cream coloured, with red and yellow lines painted on the wheel rims and spokes. The curved set of steps was down, in front of a kind of porch with a curved roof extension and carved sides. Those porch sides were a marvel. You could see through between the elements of the carvings, which were great scroll shapes around flowers and leaves and bunches of grapes. On either side of the door was a fine carriage lamp, painted red, and the door was a work of art on its own. The top half was a pair of windows with painted shutters. The bottom half was red with green and yellow painted carvings of curling vines and more grapes, and it had a letter box, she saw, with a knocker. What was a gypsy caravan doing with a letterbox? Michelle mounted the steps and looked more closely at the carvings. That yellow colour wasn't paint. It was gold leaf! She lifted the knocker and let it fall lightly.

"Come in, Michelle" called the gypsy woman from inside.

"How did you know my...?" asked the girl as she pulled the door open and found herself looking into what seemed to be an empty caravan. A movement to her left, beyond the ornate and surgically polished stove, revealed the mystery.

"Hello, Michelle. I've been expecting you. My name is Gitana" said the olive-skinned woman with the jet black hair who got up from her seat and stood facing Michelle in the narrow central aisle. She looked about 25, medium height - shorter than Michelle, at any rate - and was dressed in a manner quite foreign to Derbyshire, in a long black, red and gold skirt, white blouse and shawl of every colour in the world. She had rings and bangles and about six necklaces. Her ear-rings were large and there were pearl pins in her hair. When she moved there were flashes and glitters, as if she was somehow cloaked in tiny fairy lights which flickered at random. She was, thought Michelle, a queen of the gypsies. If what she was wearing was real, and it certainly looked it, she was the wealthiest woman in Buxton.

"Gitana, oh, well, how do you do, yes, I'm Michelle, but you know that, somehow, er..."

Michelle could see now that there was a built-in locker seat on her left, after the stove and between it and what she presumed was the bed, which went across the far end of the van. She only presumed because it was draped in all kinds of highly decorated cloths and hangings so she couldn't really tell its function. On the right was a chest of drawers, a Victorian-looking oil lamp with engraved glass bowl, and another but smaller locker seat. The gypsy woman gestured for the visitor to come forward and sit on the left-side seat, then pulled out a little folding table from under the bed.

"This is where the children should sleep" she said, "in this cupboard under the bed. But I have no children so I keep here the tools of my trade."

On the table she placed a cloth embroidered with the signs of the zodiac and other symbols which Michelle didn't recognise. On the cloth were arranged a pack of tarot cards and a pack of ordinary playing cards. A crystal ball was set on a square of black velvet. Gitana slid behind the table and sat next to Michelle.

"Now, Michelle, you have trouble in love and you want me to help. First, you must tell me what kind of trouble it is."

Michelle decided not to waste time by asking the woman how she came to be so well informed.

"I like him. In fact, I might even love him. This is odd for me, because I'm normally quite self sufficient. Even odder, I feel that I want to please him because I know he loves me. It's just..."

"You are afraid of love?"

"No, it's not that. I'm not afraid. In some ways, I think he's the one who's afraid. He's not like the others, with his hands all over you. It got to the point where I was worried he didn't like me enough to...well, you know. So I started it. I kissed him and took his hand and put it on my...here, on my chest. And when he made a response, I panicked again, like I always did before, only it wasn't fair because I'd started it. You see, it's when they touch me. I can't bear it. I have this reaction. Even with him. I want to kiss him, I want to do more than that, but I can't. I want to, but I can't, and I don't understand it! I don't understand why I want to, and I don't understand the panics."

Michelle dabbed her eyes, blew her nose and tried to compose herself.

"Michelle, this is going to be difficult" said Gitana. "You see, almost everything in my armoury is designed for the usual girl who comes to me. Girl loves boy but he doesn't love her so, she pays, I fix. Or, he loves her but she doesn't love him. He's a nuisance. He won't leave her alone. So she pays, I get rid of him for her. Or, boy used to love girl but he's cooled off a bit. She pays, I tell her how to warm him up. Or again, girl wants to love boy but can't find the right one. See what I mean? Now you come here saying boy loves girl, girl loves boy, but you can't do what you both want to do. Problem, eh?"

"It's like something between us. Ernest is too nice and too polite to say anything but he knows it's there and he won't put up with it for ever."

"No. I can see that. Well, the usual charm for drawing lovers closer together is to find a footprint of each party made in soft ground. You carefully dig up the soil that makes the footprints and put it in a pot, well mixed together. Then you plant a marigold in the pot. As the marigold grows and flowers, so the two lovers are drawn together to make one."

"Haven't you got anything a little quicker?"

"I'll think about it, Michelle, but good results don't come so fast. Quick things tend to be temporary."

"Do you think it would help if we were engaged?"

"Engaged? Has he asked you?"

"No. I don't think he will if I slap his face again. I just thought that, perhaps, if I knew we were going to be engaged, you know, it might..."

"That's easy enough. Trouble is, we can't do it now. Day after tomorrow is the full moon. Come then, at night, and we'll find out about future engagements. Meanwhile, we'll do another charm in parallel, so if we get a double result we'll be doubly sure. On the way home today, buy a lemon. Tomorrow morning, as soon as you're up, cut two pieces of peel from opposite sides of the lemon. Make the pieces about the size of a two-shilling piece. Put the pieces together, peel side out, and tie them with red thread and put your little parcel in your purse and keep it there all day. Tomorrow night, when you go to bed, take the peel out of your purse and use it to give a little rub to each leg of your bed. Touch the headboard with it, then cut the thread and put the pieces side by side, peel up, under your pillow. If you dream of him, you will marry him. What's his name?"

"Ernest."

"Ernest what?"

"Ernest Mycock."

"Michelle. Pop outside, go to the nearest bush and break off a twig. A small one, a few inches long. Bring it back here."

While Michelle did that, Gitana chose a flat piece of wood from a collection she had in a box under the bed and, with an indelible pencil, wrote 'Ernest Mycock' on it. Michelle returned with her twig.

"See where I've written his name? Take the pencil. I want you to draw a heart before his name and after it, and then tie your twig over his name, so you make a cross, with this red thread. Right. On your way home, and I suggest you go as soon as we've finished this, find a quiet spot under a tree and push this cross into the ground, among the grass and such, where it can't be seen. There are words to say which I will write out for you, and you say them kneeling in front of your cross. Then you walk away without looking back, and you repeat this for six more days. You can do your first repeat on the way here tomorrow. You are coming here tomorrow, aren't you? Yes. Good. Now, have you two sixpences? Thank you very much. Very well, these are your words."

Gitana took a postcard from a drawer and wrote on it: Opre the rooker, adre the vesh si chiriklo ta chirikli. Tele the rook, adre the vesh si piramno ta piramni.

"These are words in our language which we call Romanes. They don't translate literally but they are asking the woods and the birds to look over you and Ernest and to make you sweethearts. Thank you again for the sixpences. Bring two more tomorrow, and don't forget your lemon on the way home!

Oh, and, bring something of Ernest's. Just a small thing, a personal item."

Michelle arrived the next day, sat on the locker seat and burst into tears.

"Oh dear" said Gitana. "So you didn't dream of him, then."

"No, I didn't! I had a horrible dream instead, about water. I was in this water, and I was calling out for Ernest, and he was there but he couldn't hear me. It was awful. Frightening. He was there and I couldn't do anything."

"How very odd. He couldn't hear you? Were you swimming in the water?"

"No, not really. Not swimming like a fish or a seal. I was just sort of in it. More like a hermit crab, in his shell, in the water."

"A hermit crab? Whatever next. We'll have to think about that one. Anyway, did you remember to say your charm over the cross?"

"It's gone."

"Gone? Are you sure you..."

"Yes, yes, yes. I know exactly where I put it. I made a mental map, and I put two stones, one on either side a couple of feet away, to mark the line it was on. The stones are still there but the cross is gone."

"We'll make another. Never mind the sixpences today. I can't move on until we've had a proper trial of the cross, so we'll just have to do it all over again. Have you brought the words with you? Good. Now, go and get the twig."

For the rest of the evening and all of the next day until Michelle's appointment, Gitana felt a vague unease. Why would the cross be gone, if Michelle had hidden it properly as she said she had? There were obvious explanations. Someone, perhaps some children playing in the woods, had seen her plant the cross and had taken it for a lark. Michelle had made a mistake and looked in the wrong place. A dog had found it and made off with it, chewed it up, retrieved it. Yes, one of those had to be right.

"The cross. It's gone again." Michelle was in tears and Gitana was beginning to feel professionally stretched.

"Quite frankly, Michelle, I'm surprised you've come back. Nothing is working."

"Oh no, I don't think it's your fault. We'll find something that works. We've got to. What about the cards?"

"I'm not keen in your case. They only tell you what is likely to happen.

They don't tell you how to mend it."

"So what can we do?"

"We'll try another charm or two but I have to say I think your problem is more deep seated than I realised. We might try hypnotism, if you're agreeable."

"I'll try anything. What's first?"

"What did you bring to do with Ernest?"

"It's a tie. Just an ordinary tie. He took it off one warm day and forgot it. I keep it in a drawer. Silly, aren't I? Not the sort of thing I do."

"We'll draw the curtains...and light a candle. We'll put the tie in front of you on the table, so. Put your elbows on the table there, so that your hands are over the tie. Good. We're going to use a special gold ring as a pendulum diviner, and it is a special one, I can tell you. This gold ring is at least 150 years old and probably more. It belonged to a famous gypsy fortune teller called Rosa Faw who was privately consulted by Queen Charlotte, wife of King George III. So, you see, it ought to work. I'll just tie some red thread to the ring, and you hold the thread so that the ring hangs over the tie and just an inch or two above it. That's it. Keep your hands absolutely still. No movement at all. Now, I want you to think as hard as you can about Ernest. I want you to think about his good side, and his bad side, everything you know about him, how you met him, everything. Run the whole lot through your mind like a newsreel. It doesn't matter if you repeat bits, as long as you keep thinking about Ernest. When you've done that for a few minutes, I'll hold up a card with some Romanes words on it, and I want you to say them out loud. Right. Think away."

While Michelle thought, Gitana wrote on the card: Av, mi Romani mal, pawdel dur chumbas. Av kitane mansa?

"Are you sure your hands are perfectly still?" asked Gitana after the words had been said. Her voice had an edge to it, as if she couldn't believe what she was seeing.

"Perfectly."

The pendulum was swinging in a most irregular way. It began by moving back and forth in front of Michelle, then it moved its angle gradually until it was swinging from side to side, and it continued moving until, with its last dying swings, it had described a complete range of diameters through 360 degrees.

"Well" said Gitana. "I've never seen that before."

"What's it supposed to do?"

"Back and forth, towards you and away from you, means the signs are good for you and Ernest. Side to side means the signs are bad. Every possible angle in a complete circle means I don't know what."

"I'm sorry to be such a difficult subject, Gitana. I'm not doing it on purpose."

"No, I know you're not. We'll just have to think of something else. We'll try scrying tomorrow, with the full moon. For now, we'll try hypnosis. Is that all right?"

"What do I do?"

"Lie on the bed, that's it, climb up. Lie flat, hands clasped in front, eyes closed. I want you to listen to me very carefully. I want you to relax every part of your body, starting with your toes, now your feet, your legs, your hips, your waist, your chest, your arms, your neck, your face, your eyes. All relaxed. I want you to see in your mind that ring we used as the pendulum, the ring which belonged to Rosa Faw, the gold ring, flashing and swinging, flashing and swinging, Rosa Faw using it with Queen Charlotte. I want you to see that ring and watch it turn, catching the candlelight, flickering reflections from the flame. That ring is pure gold, pure, pure gold, and it has the ability to send you to sleep. It will send you to sleep. You're asleep now, but you can still hear my voice. All you have to do is listen to my voice and answer the questions I ask you. They'll be easy questions, Michelle. Michelle, tell me about when when you were a little girl."

Michelle didn't speak.

"Michelle" said Gitana. "In future, whenever I say to you, 'Michelle, it's the time we like', you will go to sleep as you are now. When I tap this wooden egg on the table, you will wake. But I'm not going to tap it just yet, not when you are so asleep, so deeply asleep. Now, tell me what it was like when you were a little girl."

Again there was a lengthy silence, but it was suddenly broken this time by Michelle speaking in a clear, ringing version of her own voice. It was Michelle, of course, but without her normal husky tones, without the warmth. She spoke with a cool, striking clarity, in the sound and in the words the sound shaped.

"I was of the world before. I died in this world and my spirit went in to the waters. I must keep the waters, and heal the sick, and look ever for vengeance for my death which was in great pain and before the time was due. Men must die, before their time, and many shall, before I am satisfied and paid. My waters flow from the other world and bring with them the power of fire. My waters flow warm with the power, they flow in my temple of trees, and the sun shines on the waters in the morning. Men believe they can take my power and use it, for better or for worse, but they cannot. I decide. Some men I help to live, and some I help to die. This is my fate."

Gitana sat in almost total shock. She had very little idea what was meant by Michelle's theatrical speech but she knew it was spontaneous and that it came from somewhere other than Michelle's own memory.

"Michelle, I'm going to tap the wooden egg. Wake, now!"

Michelle sat up, looking as if nothing had happened.

"I think that will do for today, Michelle. Come back tomorrow, after dark."

"What's the matter, Gitana? You look pale. Are you all right?"

"A bit of a dizzy spell. I get them sometimes. I'll be fine. I just need to lie down where you are for a while. Honestly, I'm fine. Off you go and I'll see you tomorrow."

Gitana had heard about cases like this but never had she witnessed one at first hand. They called it regression. Michelle was producing scenes from her subconscious, from beneath her subconscious possibly, which she could not have produced in her everyday, normal state of mind nor even in dreams. If the hypnotist was actively looking for signs of regression there would be no hesitation in pronouncing a triumph. Here was spectacular evidence that regression was real, to a previous life maybe, or to what?

'I was of the world before. I died in this world and my spirit went in to the waters'? What was that all about? Gitana was sympathetic to the idea of reincarnation, more than sympathetic. She could get excited about this 'proof', or she could maintain a distant, more scientific outlook and say it was nothing but a fantasy. Michelle had been to the cinema and it had sparked a lot of nonsense. She'd read a story in a magazine. 'Men must die before their time', indeed! It sounded like an extract from H Rider Haggard, or Jules

Verne. Twenty thousand leagues under the warm waters.

There was little sleep in the caravan that night. Gitana spun in her bed as she tried desperately to rid her mind of Michelle's words, every one of which seemed to have caught and held in Gitana's memory. Phrases and sentences repeated themselves over and over. Gitana could do nothing to stop them and nothing to make sense of them. Heal the sick, this is my fate, the power of fire, men must die, I decide, I decide, I decide...

It was raining as Gitana awoke from her last, shallow doze. Another grey, wet day up in the clouds in Buxton. She looked out of the window at Cody, the coloured gelding. He was unmoved by the rain, as he was unmoved by almost every circumstance. Even lightning and thunder only brought him nearer the caravan, but the grass was flattened there so he would always wander back to a lusher spot as soon as he could. At the moment, in the rain, he was applying his special philosophy. There wasn't anything he could do about the rain, so he might as well eat. Gitana called out her quiet thanks to Cody. There wasn't anything to be done about Michelle, so breakfast may as well be served.

The day dragged by, there were no other clients and the rain didn't stop until dusk. Cody assumed his customary night-time position, standing against the drystone wall by the gate where he would half-sleep until dawn, ready in position for when the farmer brought his cows in for milking. Cody liked to watch the cows go past but more particularly he liked the slice of bread the farmer always had for him. Often the farmer would have one of his children with him, generally the oldest boy who was quite capable of milking the cows himself and was much too grown-up a person to be bothered with feeding slices of bread to horses. If it was the littlest child, the farmer held her up to the gate and she thrust the bread out at Cody, her dad telling her to keep her hand flat and she squeaking with fear and fun as she felt the hairy, tickling, soft, damp mouth of Cody taking the bread away. That would be tomorrow morning, the bread. Cody didn't exactly understand the concept of tomorrow, but he knew that his was a good place to stand, to be ready, for something.

Michelle came through the gate and wondered for a moment about trying to get to know Cody, with a pat and a stroke perhaps. Looking at the horse, a statue of disinterest, she was reminded of Ernest. Cody's attitude to life's opportunities for adventure was the same as Ernest's to gypsy fortune tellers. Michelle hadn't told him precisely why she was going to Gitana, although he had probably guessed. She just said she was going out of interest, because she hadn't got her mother to talk to and needed somebody. Ernest could see the use of that but he had no time for stars and fortunes. If Michelle wanted to waste her time and money, that was fine by him but don't expect him to listen to a lot of twaddle when she came back. He would be there, ready to take her to the picture house or the well dressing at Eyam or the watercolours exhibition at Tideswell, but don't burden him with the fanciful details of a load of tripe.

Gitana placed Michelle at the table again with the crystal ball in front of her on the black velvet cloth. With the oil lamp put out, the reflected glow of the full moon was the only light in the caravan. To Michelle's right, standing in a fine silver vase of the sort designed to hold a single rose, were some unusual kind of spills or tapers. They had a thick coating on them. Gitana put a match to one and it began smouldering. She lit another. The spills gave off a smoke which smelled strongly of a perfume Michelle knew but couldn't place.

"It's a mixture" said Gitana. "Some sandalwood, some jasmine. They're called joss sticks, if you haven't seen them before. They're just for atmosphere. The Indians use them. That's where the gypsies came from originally, India. I'm going to try to get you to gaze into the crystal. It's a knack which some people can acquire and some can't. What you mustn't do is screw up your eyes and try to scry something small and far away. It's quite the opposite. You must look, but you must also relax. You must allow your eyes and your brain to become receptive. This is not a microscope you are looking into, and you're not trying to see a dot on the horizon. The crystal is a kind of reflection catcher. It holds an image for you to see, but you can only see it if you're not trying too hard. Breath deeply and slowly. Clear your mind, clear it of all pictures. The picture is in the crystal. You will see it when you are ready."

Michelle tried to do as instructed for a couple of minutes but gave up, mainly because she didn't really understand what she was aiming for.

"I don't follow you" she said. "How can I look and yet not look?"

"Have you ever seen salamanders in the fire? Have you seen faces in the soot on the fire back?"

"Well, yes, I have. I used to do that with my dad before he went to the war. He used to put half a teacake on the toasting fork and ask me where the salamander was, so he could toast the teacake in the best place. You have to look at the fire and then kind of beyond it, so it's not hot coals you're seeing but living pictures."

"And as soon as you think 'It's just coals', the dragons disappear?"

"Yes, that's it. And then we'd have the teacake with loads of butter. It was nice, doing that. I don't do it any more."

"Michelle, perhaps if you could apply the same technique, you know, looking kind of beyond it, as you say..."

After another four or five minutes, Gitana called a halt.

"We're going to try a different medium. The crystal ball is just a focus. We could use a mirror, like some of the old gypsies used and the village witches of the middle ages, or we could look into a pool of ink in my hand like the Egyptians, or a finger nail, or a sword blade. Some of the northern Red Indian tribes in America used to kill an animal and look into its liver. Liver gazing. Never done it myself but, if you can see, you can see in anything."

"Is there a point to all this?"

"The point is, Michelle, that the point is the seer, not the object used as a focus by the seer, or as a hocus-pocus for the punter. So long as it's what we call a 'clear deep'. A glass of sherry's quite a good clear deep. Amontillado, preferably."

"Are you taking me seriously, Gitana?"

"Oh yes, very. Your problem is a serious one, I can see that much, and all I'm doing is trying to show you that there are no easy answers. I get people coming here, people I don't know, expecting me to tell them if they're soon going on a long journey with a handsome stranger, or whether they're going to win the pools. If they ask idiotic questions like that, they get the idiotic methods."

"Idiotic? Are they so? What are you saying, Gitana?"

"I think I'm saying that you and I have moved beyond the Gypsy Petulengro stage. We are no longer at the seaside or the fairground. We are where the water is deep. We are behind the curtain, where we must trust each other."

Gitana went over to the small locker seat, lifted the lid and pulled something out.

"Conch shell. For shell-hearing, which is like crystal gazing only in sound. You might as well try and tune your wireless to Honolulu for all the good that will do. And here we have tarot cards. How can anybody seriously believe that shuffling a pack of cards can tell the future? I mean, what forces are supposed to be acting here? Who or what is arranging the cards in order? Complete rubbish. Like throwing dice, or bones, or expecting to see the future in tea leaves and two magpies."

"But you had tarot cards out when I first came."

"When you first came, I assumed you would be just another silly girl with a crush on some boy. That's what they usually are. A silly girl who wants me to cast a spell on a boy so he'll be devoted and worship at her feet and not go running around after all the other silly girls. So I cast a spell, or read the cards, or whatever. That's what they want, so that's what I give them."

On the chest of drawers by the window was a ceramic hand, a cream-coloured pottery hand which stood, as it were, on its wrist. It had lines and symbols on it, marked in black. Gitana picked it up and waved it at Michelle.

"See this? Palmistry. Rubbish."

"I thought a lot of people believed in palmistry."

"They do, Michelle, so they do. But I have yet to see a gypsy ask another gypsy for a palm reading. The palmist is a natural, instinctive psychologist we might say, full of the tricks passed down through gypsy generations, but she's not using the palm to get her ideas."

"I've got a long life line." Michelle proffered her hand.

"So have I, but I'm not counting on it. I notice you also have a large mountain of Venus, here at the ball of your thumb, which is to do with charitable inclinations and enthusiastic love of your fellow man - in every possible way, that is, including what they used to call libertinage but what the Americans now call sleeping around. The bigger your mountain of Venus, the keener you are on giving yourself to every man's favourite charity. You could also say it represented the amount of work you do with your hands, since the ball of your thumb is just a muscle and like any other you can develop it with exercise."

"Such as clearing tables and carrying tea trays."

"Exactly."

"What are the other mountains?"

"They're named after planets. Jupiter, Mercury, Mars. And there's the Sun and Moon."

"Where's that? The Moon, I mean?"

"Here, just above your heart line."

"And what does it stand for?"

"A big juicy mountain of the Moon means you are sensitive to the needs of others and you're a fine upstanding citizen of the world. An itsy-bitsy miserable one means you are thoroughly immoral, bad tempered and selfish, or, it could mean you are a dainty-pawed, lightly-built gentlewoman whose hobbies are listening to the BBC and watching the grass grow."

"So you don't reckon a lot to palmistry, even though you practise it."

"I practise it because it makes good money and people expect it of me. In fact, the hand is a mechanical device for gripping, made of bones, muscles, skin, tendons and so on, and what it looks like depends on the bones, muscles and whatnot you were given by your ancestors and what you have given your hands to do during your life so far. I'll provide you with a quotation, if I may. I can't remember where it's from, but it struck me forcibly when I was younger and studying such things with an open mind. Ahem. 'That these purely mechanical arrangements of the hand have any psychic, occult or predictive meaning is a fantastic imagination which seems to have a peculiar attraction for a certain type of mind. Its discussion does not lie within the province of reason.' You could apply that quotation to a lot of my stuff, actually. Hardly any of it lies within the province of reason."

"Don't you believe in any supernormal powers at all? I mean, what are you doing all this for, if not?"

"I'll tell you someday. And yes, I do believe, which is what I'm worried about in your case. Anyway, where was I? Ah yes, we were going to see if you can see, which is a matter for belief I assure you. And we are going to do it using one of the best media for a beginner."

Gitana brought out a half-pint beer glass, a perfectly straight-sided cylinder, which she filled to the very top with water.

"Not just any old water, either. Buxton spring water. Very pure, been under the ground for thousands of years. We'll have a candle for more light, and we'll have more joss sticks. Now, start gazing. Look into the top of the glass, down into the water. Remember. Deep, slow breaths. Relax. Don't peer or stare or try too hard. Allow your sense of sight to flow into the water."

After a few moments, Michelle gave a little shriek and flapped her hands about, sending glass and water flying across the caravan.

"Oh, I'm sorry, Gitana. Sorry. I had a bit of a shock."

"What kind of a shock?"

"I was doing what you said, allowing myself to kind of float on the water, and suddenly there was a picture. It was a girl. Like me. Only she was dead. Killed, I mean. Murdered. There was blood. And she was naked, this girl."

"What do you mean, like you? How like you was she? Was she like you in age? Colouring? Figure?"

"She was like me in every way. Very like me, in fact. I should say she was me. Oh, Gitana! What does this mean? Does it mean I'm going to be killed?"

"Shouldn't think so. No, not at all. More likely, it means you were killed, once" said Gitana, trying to make light of it but remembering the words of the day before. 'I died in this world. I must look ever for vengeance for my death in great pain. Men must die...'

"I beg your pardon?" asked Michelle.

"In a previous existence. You met a bad end in a life before this one. Somehow the memory of it hasn't faded entirely away. You called it back and saw it in the water."

"Reincarnation? You don't believe in the cards but you do believe in reincarnation?"

"Most certainly. Now, that's enough for one day, quite enough. Come again tomorrow and we'll try the hypnosis again. Something is troubling your inner spirit and we must get to the cause of it and let it out."

The instant Michelle was gone, Gitana made up a strong sleeping draught. It was a mixture of her own, following an old herbal recipe but with the addition of a more widely available and less secret ingredient, a triple whisky. It generally worked, even on nights of high stress.

Next day was a normal day in the cafe but Michelle felt anything but normal. These sessions with Gitana were becoming addictive. She couldn't wait for the day to go by.

"Michelle, it's the time we like. What do you remember, Michelle?"

"Some men have come to me, new men, different men. They have found my warm waters for the first time and they are astonished. They are fearful, too. They wonder if the water is made warm by magic. It seems they are an advance party, a warring faction of a tribe of men. They have driven the other men away who used to be here, the men who used to honour me. The new men await their elders and chiefs. They come, the elders. There are priests among them, druids, who see a chance to make their own positions stronger. They tell the chiefs and the other men that the waters are made warm by a goddess, and that they, the druids, are the only ones who know how to deal with this goddess. I laugh at that, and my springs bubble. The men are more afraid. The druids take command, with great presence of mind. They are clever among men, these druids, but they are no match for me. I look into their souls and I see how black and wrinkled some of them are. Their souls are like the black berries on the bramble tree when it is winter and they are shrivelled and dry. I will have my vengeance upon them. I despise all priests. Let them try their petty tricks on me and we shall see what happens. Men! I shall decide what happens to men!"

"Michelle, I'm tapping the egg, now!"

"Well?" Michelle asked. "What news from the far country?"

"I shouldn't mock too much if I were you, Michelle. Tell me, what do you know about the Ancient Britons, the Celts?"

"We did them at school. Boadicea and all that, and the Romans. Then the Anglo Saxons came and beat them in battle and pushed them into Wales. Something of the sort."

"And that's all you know?"

"Why would I want to know any more? Who wants to know about funny little Welsh gnomes living in the hills? What's all this for, Gitana? Is there a point?"

"Do you know what regression is, Michelle?" The gypsy woman stared hard at her client, looking for the slightest telltale.

"Course I do. I was top in English. Regression is going backwards."

"Hypnotists use the term to mean going back to a previous life. Under the influence, you see, in a perfectly relaxed state, the theory is that you regress to an existence you have otherwise blanked out. I suppose we blank out these existences on the grounds that, if we could remember all our previous lives all the time, we'd be too confused to get on with this one."

"Surely that's a load of nonsense, Gitana? You don't expect me to believe..."

"I'll tell you what, Michelle. If I could afford one of those recording machines and I had recorded you five minutes ago, you wouldn't be talking like this."

"So who did I regress to? Sorry, whom. Top in English. To whom did I regress? I hope it was somebody who had a good time."

"Another theory is that you're not actually regressing to a real past life of your own, but rather you are somehow tuning in to evidence of the past that is still around you but so faint that normally you can't see it or hear it. You're like an extra-sensitive radio receiver set, picking up signals sent years ago. The same theory applies to ghosts, you know, that they're not actually ghosts but rather the past replaying itself, like a kind of psychic moving picture at an invisible cinema which you occasionally walk into by accident."

"What, you mean that every little thing that happened in the past is still floating about somewhere?"

"That's what they say. It's all too faint for almost everyone, because they go around with their supernatural radio receivers permanently off. But certain special people can see it when they are hypnotised so their normal sensory barriers are down and their secret valves are humming."

"So what did I see? Come on, Gitana! Spill the beans, as they say in the non-psychic moving pictures."

Gitana refused to spill any beans in case the knowledge spoiled what might come next from a hynotised Michelle. They agreed to have a daily session for a week. If there seemed to be more to find, they would continue. If not, Gitana would tell all and together they would see what they could make of it.

The next day, Gitana allowed Michelle to go on for longer, as she seemed to want to get to the end of a story.

"What do you remember, Michelle?"

"They have felled all the trees, the men, for miles about, so they can farm the land, but they know they must leave a home of trees for their goddess of the warm spring. In the centre, near the spring herself, is the biggest tree of all, a great oak tree, and other trees are left to stand at careful distances, so that in summer time their branches in leaf join together and form a roof of green which is the roof of my temple. On the edge of my circle of trees they allow hazels to grow, to make a hedge around, and they make a gateway and a long clearing to the east, so that the morning sun shines on the way to my spring and on the spring herself. They have built a wall of stones so that my spring makes a deep pool and is contained in a circle. Travellers come to pay their respects at my pool, and throw small valuables into it, pieces of copper and silver, even gold sometimes, and once or twice they have thrown in jewellery. They believe that this will bring them good fortune. They also believe that to take something from the pool will surely bring them ill. That much at least is true, for I shall not tolerate a man taking something from me. No matter how poor and desperate he may be, if he steals from me a little thing, he shall die. They believe in the good, the men, that they think comes of offering me their pieces of metal, and they know for certain of the bad that comes from thieving. Inside my grove which they have made, at the end of the long clearing, certain trees have been felled so that an open space is there, where the druids can gather and make their ceremonies. Fools! They think their sacrifices and offerings can influence me! I can cure them or curse them, raise them up or knock them down, as I wish. I decide. I decide!"

Michelle was becoming agitated again. Gitana tapped the wooden egg.

"Do you think this is getting me anywhere with Ernest?" asked Michelle.

"Reasonable question. Answer, don't know. Probably not, and we should probably stop now but, I confess to you, I feel that when the mist clears I shall discover America. It's like that. I don't know what's going to happen but I need to find out. Perhaps we shall soon get to the end of the regression and then you, the hypnotised you, will allow me to start trying to deal with your present day problems."

"What? I'm still regressing? Same person?"

"Yes. The same, er, person. See you tomorrow?"

With no results, no progress and no promise of any, Michelle's logical side told her that any more hypnotism was a waste of time. It is in the nature of an addict to hide away from logic, thus making it disappear.

"Two sisters are coming to my spring. They walk hand in hand, talking and laughing. I see they are both beautiful, but one is older and her beauty will fade the sooner. It will fade the faster also because there is evil in her soul. She talks and laughs with her younger sister but all the time intends to do her the worst harm. They kneel beside my pool. The elder sister gives a great blow to the younger with a stone from my pool! From my pool! The kneeling girl falls flat to the ground. Quickly the elder drags her unconscious form into my pool and holds her head under my spring waters until she is dead. Then, the evil one takes a gold pin from her hair and stabs her dead sister once in each eye. Blood mixes with water on her beautiful white face as she is dragged to the trees and left there, to be recovered later, at night. I see this has all been done for love. The elder and the younger both loved the same man, where he came to woo the elder only and loved her but gradually came to love the younger more. Now the younger is gone, vanished into the air, he cannot love her and so there is no obstacle to the wedding. It will be held soon. The bride-to-be comes at night with a horse and takes her dead sister away, to bury her in a bog. Nothing now stands in the way of her happiness in this life. At the wedding, a lovely young blind girl is playing music for the feast on a harp, and while she is playing she begins to sing. Her song tells the wedding guests how she was taken to Arnemetia's spring and there was beaten and drowned and stabbed in the eyes, and taken away to be buried in a bog. The bridegroom hears the song and is struck dumb with horror. The bride stands up, paler than a lily, trembling more than any harp string. The holy man says that since they have not had union of their flesh, their marriage can be declared as nought. The groom silently agrees. The bride flees to the river. She ties her feet together and gives a poor man money to persuade him to tie her hands together also. She throws herself in the river and is drowned and her soul flows upstream, against the current, to the north, where the evil of the world is stored."

The wooden egg was tapped and tea was served.

"Gitana. I have something to say."

"You want to stop the sessions."

"No, it's not that. In fact, it's kind of opposite to that. The thing is, I don't understand why I don't want to stop the sessions. We don't seem to be getting anywhere. It seems to be more for your benefit than mine. You don't tell me anything about what's been happening. Yet I still feel I want to come back."

"All right, Michelle. I promise I'll tell you soon. It's just that I have feelings about it too. I feel that I am drawing something out of you, and when it's all gone, you will be free of it and able to be, well, Michelle."

"Normal, you mean."

"Michelle. You came to me because of you and Ernest. It wasn't working like you imagined it should. You felt pressure. You felt pressure from Ernest, although he never expressed it, and pressure from yourself, because you were not like the other girls. What I am hoping to do is resolve these problems. I think we're nearly there. Look, take a few days off. Go out with Ernest somewhere. Come back here, let's say next Tuesday. We'll have three more sessions on the trot, Tuesday, Wednesday, Thursday. Then, I'll tell you all about it and with any luck we'll have done the job."

Tuesday soon came. Michelle was feeling well and strong. They'd been for a long walk on the Saturday afternoon, had the usual gigantic Sunday lunch, the cafe had been frantic all Monday and Tuesday with trips of visitors and the time had flown. She jumped on to Gitana's bed and settled down.

"Michelle, it's the time we like. What do you remember?"

"The druids have come with three maidens. The maidens are lying in a bed which is carried by the druids. They set it down in a central place near my spring and walk around the bed casting flowers and herbs upon the maidens. The druids think all this silliness will influence me. It will, but not in the way they think. When they have walked around the bed seven times, they sit on the ground and the chief among them begins to tell a story. I have heard this story many times over the ages, since I was flung from the world, and all of these druids have heard it too. But they listen. I have heard it so often that I could correct the druid when he goes wrong, if I thought it worthwhile in the slightest to do so. The story has a special, deep significance which escapes me but means much to them. It concerns a great warrior-king's son. This son, called Arrawn, did not excel with the sword or the axe or the bow or the spear, as the king his father had, but rather at games of bowls. He was a disappointment to his father but no-one could beat him at bowls. One day, a very old man came and offered to play bowls with the king's son. Everybody laughed, but the old man said he had a wager. The winner of the game could ask anything he liked of the loser, and the loser must perform as asked or die. Arrawn laughed again and said he would please the old man who, of course, then won the game of bowls. The task he set Arrawn was to be finished in no more space than a year. In that time, Arrawn had to find out the old man's name and the situation of his house. That was the task. Instantly, the old man went away and was gone. Arrawn set off the next day and after many weeks' travel came upon another very old man, who said he was two hundred years old and the elder brother of the bowls player. The bowls player, the very old man said, was called Green Sleeves. Now all Arrawn had to do was find the house. The elder brother sent Arrawn two hundred thousand paces to find yet another, even older man, the eldest brother of the three, who was four hundred years old. This brother sent Arrawn four hundred thousand paces to a river where swam three swans. One of these swans had a blue wing. When they came out of the water they cast aside their feathers and were revealed as beautiful young women, naked to the sky. While they were brushing their hair, Arrawn stole the feathers of the blue winged swan so that when she came for her feathers to dress in, they were gone. Arrawn offered them back to her, provided she helped him, to which she agreed. She took him to the castle where her father lived, and he was the old man who had won at bowls. The old man said that Arrawn had cheated in his tasks and would be killed unless he completed three more tasks. The three new tasks were, one, to build a castle a thousand thousand paces in length with stones from every quarry in the land; two, to take flax seed from a cask, sow it, reap it, thresh it and return it to its cask, all in a single day; and three, to clean out the castle stables, which had not been touched for a thousand years, and there find a golden needle which had been lost nine hundred and ninety nine years before. Blue Wing helped him achieve all of this. Later, the two were married and when his own father died, Arrawn ruled as king in peace for many years. So, the druid has finished his tale and the others are bringing the maidens from the bed. The maidens have no clothing but the flowers and feathers in their hair. They are bound hand and foot, but not too tightly, and they know what they have to do. They have to walk to my pool. They are to do this without stumbling, and they are to kneel and take my sacred waters with a kiss. One of them manages to do it. The other two stumble and are swiftly taken and tied into the bed. They weep and wail in their fear. The druids pile straw and wood around the bed and set it alight. I promise the druids that one day they will know what it is like to be consumed by flames. This is the result of their sacrifices. This is their influence. I look on such men with contempt and make a vow to avenge the innocents. The two maidens die in the fire, the maidens who stumbled. The other, who will become a priestess, looks on."

Michelle fell silent. Gitana looked at her in a kind of admiring fear. How much more of this truly dreadful material was there to come? Next day, she would find out.

"There is great trouble among men. It is no concern of mine when men slay each other for no purpose, but this time there are innocents being killed. The men called Corieltauvi have come up from the south and have given battle to the men called Brigantes, who are the men who live beside me. I know this because the druids have been to ask for my help in the battle, which is not something they would normally ask. Usually they want me to heal their wounded, not fight their fights for them, and so I must believe that times are desperate in their eyes. They say it is bad because the best fighters of the Brigantes are away to the north, giving battle to more men who are called Parisi. Men are very stupid, and fight and kill each other simply because they live in a different place and call themselves by a different name, when in every important respect they are all identical and there is no cause for any difference between them. It has happened that the Brigantes left at home are defeated by the invading Corieltauvi, and the Corieltauvi have brought twelve of the young Brigantes women to my grove. Most of these women have clear souls, but regardless of that they are speared upon wooden stakes which are thrust into them from below, where their nether limbs meet, and further thrust until the sharpened end appears from the shoulder beside the neck, where their upper limbs meet. Still they are not dead, and the last one to be impaled has watched and heard eleven others treated thus, and the first is alive to see and hear all the other eleven. They die now in the most terrible agony. The men of the Brigantes return from the north and find this circumstance, and they are filled with wrath, and they slay many of the Corieltauvi and pursue the rest to their own country and there take revenge on the women and children. When they come home they are ashamed. They have wrought unspeakable evil on the Corieltauvi. They ask for my forgiveness and they wash in my spring. Why should I favour them? It was men who speared the clear-souled women, and men who ask for forgiveness. I am not interested in their begging. Even the waters of my spring cannot wash clean their souls."

Gitana was very tempted to end the whole business there and then, to ask Michelle to leave and never come back, to harness Cody to the living waggon and head for sunnier climes. Perhaps she would do that tomorrow. No, the day after. She would hold the last session, tell Michelle a little of what had happened, and go. She might go to the coast. Somewhere civilised. She might set off for north Norfolk. There wouldn't be any Celtic goddesses in north Norfolk, surely. Yes, tomorrow would be the last day.

"The wise men are here, and among them is the one they call The Physician, who is supposedly the most skilled at invoking my powers to heal the sick. The wise men bring with them a soldier, a Roman officer, who has been wounded in battle against the Pictish. I know this Roman. He is strong among men. He has killed many in the wars and has put women and children to the sword. I can see this in his soul, which is greatly weakened and discoloured by his deeds. The Physician begins to say spells and to cast herbs into my spring. He says they number among them every healing herb in the land, which they might well do for all I care. You see, I am not listening to this fool. I am instead thinking of another Roman, a citizen, not a soldier, a kind and gentle man called Aelius Motio who looked after his family and his servants and who came to me with a sick daughter. She was very sick indeed but not yet near to death. Often men come to me when all is almost lost, as a last resort, when nothing else has helped. These men, sometimes I smile upon them and sometimes I do not. Aelius Motio came to me in plenty of time, knowing that the sickness was very bad but not waiting until his daughter was terribly damaged and only hours from her death. I listened to the prayers of Aelius. I saw that he truly had his faith in me. He put gold in my spring and promised to make an altar to me. The gold meant nothing to me but I understood the strength of the gesture. I looked into the soul of his daughter and saw that it was clear, like my spring. A clear soul makes the task of healing so much easier and less exhausting. The daughter of Aelius Motio, called Cassia, was made well and she was destined to live happily. There is an altar now, made to me at Navio where this family lived. He named me a goddess on the altar, which is how men think of me. They do not really comprehend what I am. They do not understand the Law of Three, how it goes around. The maid, the mother, the crone. Life, death and rebirth. The fall, the blossom, the fruit. The maid, the mother, the crone. I am outside the short cycle men know, which they try to measure and divide into even smaller pieces of time as if it were a rope or a distance to run at the games, but I still obey the Law. Men would be happier if they saw how time goes around and around, not along in a line. Now the one called The Physician is crying out to me in loud cries. He chants a holy spell, one of their secrets which, like all such, means nothing. I look at the Roman soldier's soul and I see there is no hope for him, not even if I wanted to save him. Greater powers than I have already decided where he shall go. I laugh at The Physician and my spring bubbles up a little more strongly. They thank me. They think the soldier is saved. But I know he is not. He will be dead tomorrow."

Gitana tapped the wooden egg and Michelle sat up as usual, but this was not to be the usual session ending. Gitana had decided to tell, and to quit.

"Michelle" said Gitana, "I don't quite know how to say this but somehow you seem to have tuned in to the life, if you can call it that, of an Ancient British goddess."

Michelle opened her mouth to speak but Gitana kept going.

"Don't ask me how or why. I haven't got a clue. For a start, believing it means admitting that there were, or are, such beings as goddesses, and that it is possible for a human being to blend into one of them. Or, it could mean admitting that you can communicate over the barrier of death, possibly over thousands of years, with an Ancient Briton, a Celt, possibly a druid, who believed in the goddess and knew all about her. Or, if we can take it as far as it will go, it means that you have in you a spirit which was in a goddess all those aeons ago. Just a moment, while I make a cup of tea."

"Tea? Surely goddesses don't drink tea? What do they drink, goddesses? I'll have some, anyway." Michelle felt herself felt herself gripped by a type of hysteria. She was suddenly operating at a different level. Like a mother who has been told that her child has a fatal illness, she defended the impossibility of it all by attacking.

"Michelle" said Gitana, worried by the reaction. "Don't take this so lightly. And please shut up for a moment while I collect my thoughts."

With the tea made and poured, Gitana had her line worked out.

"Right, my girl. What do you know about Celtic religion?"

"Nothing."

"Have you ever heard of Arnemetia?

"Arnie who?"

"Treating your flippancy with the contempt it deserves, allow me to give you a lesson in Ancient British. In their language, 'Ar' means 'at', 'nemet' means 'grove' or, more probably here, 'sacred grove', since we know that some of the British used to worship in the open air rather than in temples, and often in a grove, which is to say a little wood or group of trees giving shelter or, in this case, forming a natural meeting place, sorry, I'm rather rabbiting on a bit, aren't I? The ending of the word, 'ia', shows that it's a name and a female one. Arnemetia. She at the grove."

"She at the grove? You're saying I'm a goddess and they call me she at the grove? It sounds like gossip over the garden wall. You know, her that lives at Number Five. Is that my name, she at the grove?"

"That's literally it. If we assume that the grove is a holy place, then it's more likely to be she who is of the sacred grove, or she who lives at the, er..."

"Her at Number Five, Sacred Grove, Buxton, Derbyshire. I thought it was going to be exciting, being a goddess, but I'm just a girl who lives in a tree."

"It's not just any girl, or any tree. The Romans named Buxton after you."

"Oh, right. Bux Ton. The town of the ape girl."

"No, no, no. Please, calm down and take this with a bit more...it's a very grave matter."

"Fine. I'll be grave about the grove."

"Michelle! Will you please stop it and listen! The Roman name for Buxton was Aquae Arnemetiae, which simply means 'the waters of Arnemetia'. So, when they got here and built their fort, they called the place after its most important and already established inhabitant. You. Or rather, should I say, the goddess Arnemetia. That is, if she was a goddess. She might just have been a nymph or minor figure inhabiting the spring and looking after it, or she might have been the spring itself, or rather herself."

"Herself?"

"As you obviously knew when you were hypnotised, springs were thought of as being female. Anyway, it could have started off either way. The Ancient British may have believed that the spring was holy, because it came out of the ground warm, or that it was made warm and holy by supernatural intervention. Either way, they had to have a goddess. And, somehow, you,

Michelle Mercer, two thousand years later, when we have King George and Clement Attlee instead of Caesar Augustus, seem to be involved. So, there you are."

"And that's it and all about it?"

"If you mean can I do anything more, no, I can't. The sessions don't lead anywhere or do anything for the original problem. I think they may even be doing more harm than good. Your gypsy woman hereby withdraws her services. Tomorrow morning, I'm going."

"You can't do that! It's you who got me into this. What am I going to do without you? Gitana!"

"I hope you will return to a normal kind of life. In any case, stay away from hypnotists. Michelle, it has been quite an experience and I think we have become friends. But, it's time to move on. Now, if you will excuse me, I have some packing to do."

CHAPTER FOUR

VERY little packing was done, due to Gitana's hard facade collapsing the moment Michelle left, so that she spent the night weeping, thinking, going around in mad circles and drinking whisky. Next day, mid morning, by which time she had planned to be on the road, she and her caravan were still there for Ernest to find.

It did not take a great deal of appealing to Gitana's better side to prevent the departure, at least for now. Michelle had been inconsolable and thoroughly depressed and Ernest, although he didn't say so directly, thought it was all Gitana's doing. There was a responsibility here. Walking out on it was not the right thing to do.

"Come in to the caravan, Ernest, and sit down. I will agree to carry on for a few more sessions but I will not do it alone. You must be here. I need your strength and you need to see for yourself. Will you do that? Very well, Ernest, can I ask you, how are you disposed towards mystical things? I mean religion, magic, ghosts, spirits, anything like that?"

"I go to church on a Sunday, but that's more out of convention than anything else. Actually, I can't say I've thought very deeply about it. I suppose I do have a general belief in God, or a god, but I'm not going to believe every word in the Bible. Saints, miracles, Genesis, no. Supreme being or beings, a careful yes. How's that for a red hot answer?"

"It's a good answer. I was hoping you'd be fairly neutral, because I want you to look and listen to what will happen when Michelle is here, and I want you to do it as a non believer. I want you to apply your disinterested, logical, even cynical brain to an illogical and totally impossible phenomenon."

"What on earth are you on about? Michelle said you hypnotised her. It's an accepted medical practice. Lots of them do it."

"But it's what happens when I hypnotise her. The thing is, because she doesn't remember any of it when she comes out, I am the only witness so far. I have given her a few clues about what goes on, but you will be an independent person to see and hear it too, to be there when she...travels."

"Travels? Where to?"

"Look, Ernest, please don't take this wrongly. It is quite impossible, what I'm going to tell you, but you must at least believe that I think I have witnessed it. When she is hypnotised, Michelle appears to become one of the old pre-Roman goddesses, called Arnemetia."

"I've heard of her. Goddess of Buxton. Of the springs or something. How can Michelle know anything about her?"

"That's it. She doesn't. She claims never to have heard the name. In her normal state of mind, awake, conscious, she knows nothing of the Celts, the Ancient Brits, the Iron Agers, whatever you want to call them, or their religion. She has no information and nothing to say on the subject. Yet, when she is hypnotised, she knows the most intimate details and recounts the most breathtaking stories as if she were there, watching it all happen. She also seems to know the classical folk tales, the really old ones. Green Sleeves, the two sisters, that kind of thing. These stories appear in all sorts of different traditions. They were handed down from prehistoric times but they stopped long before they got to twentieth century Buxton."

"Maybe she's heard about it somewhere and she's faking."

"I really don't think so, although what you say is possible. You see, some of what she comes out with doesn't appear in any book she'd be likely to read. For example, how many books are there in Buxton Library describing human sacrifices in pre-Roman Britain?"

"It doesn't matter how many there are. I know for a fact that Michelle has never even been inside Buxton Library. She's not a bookish person. She likes the films. She likes the moving pictures."

"Certainly what she tells me in her sleep is a moving picture, but her language is very literate. Bookish, even. She sounds sort of biblical, almost. It's formal, as if it was written and not recently. So, Ernest, if she doesn't read, how else would she hear about it?"

"I don't know. It depends where these things are talked about."

"Specialised departments in universities. Secret meetings of pagan societies. Obscure gatherings of advanced students of folk tale and legend."

"Oh, I see. Not the Bakers Arms in West Road, then."

"No, not the Bakers. Nor, I would suggest, any other pub in Buxton."

"You get quite a few pagans in the Swan. And legends. But I see what you mean. If Michelle made no special effort to discover all this, and I can't even imagine she would have the first idea of where to start, we can say we know she would be most unlikely just to stumble across it."

"Exactly. Now, look out. She'll be here in a minute."

"How do you know that? She was asleep on our couch when I last saw her."

The subject came into the hynotist's consulting rooms, or Michelle opened the door of the caravan and stepped inside.

"I came to see if you would really leave. I'm so glad you've stayed. What are you doing here, Ernest?"

"He's here because I invited him, Michelle. I need him to help me help you. Now, do you want to get on? Good. In your usual place, please. Ernest, you must promise me that whatever happens, you will not utter a word nor try to communicate with Michelle in any way. Promise? Michelle is an extremely good subject for hypnosis and I can put her under simply by saying 'Michelle, it's the time we like'. There, you see, she is asleep. It's called post hynotic suggestion, Ernest. Under hypnosis previously, I told her that she would sleep whenever she heard me say that sentence. I chose a sentence someone else is unlikely to say, just as a precaution. Now, I'm going to ask her a few questions. Usually I only have to say 'What do you remember?' and she's away. This time I am going to be more specific. Michelle. Where is your grove?"

"My grove is by the river. My springs rise near the river but they are not to do with it. The river has its own spirit and its own destiny. My springs come from deep in the earth. The river merely flows over its surface."

"Does the river have a name?"

"A name? Why would it have a name? Names are given by men. They give names to springs, not to the channels which do no more than carry water to the sea."

"Can you see into the future?"

"I can see some things, but not everything."

"Can you see what will happen to your grove?"

"Yes, I can see that. Men who have forgotten me will come and cut down my grove. They will build a great building where my grove stood. It will be a vast enterprise, this building, unlike anything that can be comprehended. It will be of stone, stone that has been cut into perfect shapes, and it will present the form of a pair of bulls' horns. It will have many openings through which men can see but not pass. And the men will do an unimaginable thing to the river, so that they can walk and build upon it."

"What will happen to your springs?"

"My springs will be safe. They will always be safe. Men will care for my springs because my springs care for men. Men will become wealthy through my springs. Men might forget me but they cannot forget a way to wealth. I weep for my grove, which is cut down and burned after so many years in the affairs of men. I laugh because men cause my warm spring to come from a stone well which they name for a goddess who has never existed."

"Michelle, I want you to stay asleep for a while. You will not be able to hear anything at all until I say 'Michelle' three times running. So, Ernest, what do you make of that?"

"I don't know, Gitana. I really don't. If I were a stranger, I'd say she was a fraud. She's heard somewhere about St Anne. Michelle knows it's called St Anne's Well. Everybody knows that."

"I'll ask her in a minute. What do you know about St Anne, Ernest?"

"Not much. I tried to find out, once. To do with a book I was working on. Oh yes, I've got quite a few ideas for books. I'll finish one, one day. Yes, St Anne doesn't appear in the Bible but she's supposed to be the mother of the Virgin Mary."

"Quite so. If you go to All Saints church in York you will see her in a stained glass window and I think there's a painting of her in the National Gallery, but those are probably the most substantial things there are about her. Somebody, somewhere, made her up."

"The Virgin Mary must have had a mother."

"Even if her son didn't have a father, you mean? Yes, of course she had a mother, but nobody knows who she was. There is no historical record. Yet there is all this about St Anne who was supposed to be Jesus' grandmother, and Emerentiana, his great grandmother, and Stollius his great grandfather, and Anne's sister Esmeria who was mother of Elizabeth and so grandmother of John the Baptist, et cetera et cetera. Nonsense, all of it."

"You seem to know your subject rather well."

"For an illiterate gyppo? Yes, quite, but I'm not, you see. I'm not a gypsy fortune teller. I mean, my real name's McLennan. Not a very gypsy name. No, I'm more of a scholar of the old religions. A priestess, you might say."

"What? Dancing naked in the woods?"

"On occasion. When there's a full moon, an R in the month and a nice plump baby to eat. I'll let you know when we're doing it next."

"Sorry. I shouldn't mock something I know nothing about. Sorry."

"Quite. I tell fortunes to make a living, Ernest, and I pretend to be a gypsy and I live in a caravan because that way nobody asks any questions. Please keep my secret or they'll have me proclaimed a witch and burnt at the stake, or put on the train to Stockport."

"Your secret is safe with me, provided you promise not to turn me into a newt. Sorry. Sorry again. All right. The matter in hand. I agree it's unlikely that Michelle would know any details about St Anne, the goddess who never existed, but it is possible. However, knowing her, I would say she could not have known about the trees being cut down when they built the Crescent, and running the River Wye underground in a conduit. I mean, I only know because I'm interested in Buxton history. I don't suppose one in a hundred Buxton people know when the Crescent was built, much less what was there before it."

"Let's see, shall we? Michelle, Michelle, Michelle, what is the name of the goddess after whom the men of the future will call your springs?"

"I don't know her name. How can I know her name if she has never existed?"

"Why will men change their faith from you to her?"

"To please a king. A king among men has a wife...this is not very clear. Men shall find a figure, carved in oak, of a woman and child. It is an offering to me. It is supposed to be me. I know where it is now. It is in my pool. It lies beside all the coins they throw, and the worthless bracelets and other adornments they make from metal. What need have I for money and metal decorations? They think that what is of value to them is of value to me. One day, men will find this supposed likeness of me and the coins and other trash, and at last they will remember me again, but they will not believe because they have forgotten how to believe. They will think the likeness is a plaything, an object to wonder at and talk about, when really it is Arnemetia."

"Arnemetia? A woman with a child? Have you had a child?"

"Of course not. Your understanding is poor. The figure is Arnemetia. The child is sick, the child is of the man who carved the oak. He wants the child to live and commends it to my care with his offering. I will decide if it lives. I will decide."

"What will they call the building which will be set in place of your grove?"

"I don't know the name. It has no name yet, not until it is built. It will be in the shape of a new moon."

"What will they do to the river?"

"They do not want the river to be there, but they cannot stop it flowing. It will not be contained, and so they will place the earth above it and let it flow."

"What is the name your springs go by?"

"Arnemetia."

"Is that your name too?"

"I am the springs, and the springs are my name."

"Michelle, I want you to stay asleep for a while. You will not be able to hear anything at all until I say 'Michelle' three times running. So, again, Ernest, what do think is going on?"

"The king was Richard the Second. Married Anne of Bohemia. It is said among the wise that our burghers of Buckstones christened our well after the queen, to honour her virtue and perfect distinction, or, perhaps, to creepy-creep a little into the king's favour. But what's that about a statue?"

"Don't know about that. There was a story of a stone statue being found which was thought to have had ANNE carved on it but which actually was a misreading of ARNE for Arnemetia, but the story never got very far, presumably because there never was a statue really to back it up. And Michelle said oak, which is more likely than stone. Which reminds me. In your historical studies, have you ever come across a Roman citizen, local to here, called Aelius Motio?"

"Don't think so. Why?"

"Will you do me a favour, Ernest? See if you can find a reference to this man, in connection with Arnemetia."

"Aelius Motio. Will do. And what about the coins?"

"Standard practice, Ernest. Coins in the fountain, coins in the wishing well, coins in the sacred spring. People have done it ever since they had coins to throw. The technical term is votive, something offered in the hope of. Somewhere in Buxton there'll be a stack of votive coins, waiting to be dug up. Under the baths, I shouldn't wonder." Gitana paused and looked hard at Ernest. "So, Ernest the Cynic. What do you reckon?"

"Well, I can't understand it, I can't see how it works, but it's obvious that something strange is going on. I would have sworn that Michelle had never heard of Anne of Bohemia or had the slightest notion about statues, coins, holy springs, sacred groves, whatever. Any of it. I think, probably, I don't actually want to understand it. I think it might be best left alone."

"I agree. I have told her a little about Arnemetia but only as much as she could have found out for herself. I have made notes of what she has said, and I intend to write them up as a study into a phenomenon, part of my work, no more. No mention of real names, naturally. But I think it's time to call a halt to this. I don't see that it can lead us anywhere which could be useful to Michelle. I came across it by accident, and I'll leave it on purpose. Yes?"

"Yes."

"Michelle, Michelle, Michelle. You can hear me now. I am going to tap the wooden egg and you will be awake. There, now, how do you feel?"

"Fine. As always. I have had an idea, though."

"An idea? What sort of idea?"

"I thought I might try and get a job at the hot baths. You know, near my spring. It seems sort of logical."

Ernest shifted uneasily while Gitana tried to stay perfectly calm.

"Did you say your spring? You know that's not possible."

"Did I? Slip of the tongue. No, I just feel I would like a job at the baths. Better than at the grocer's, anyway, and I'm a bit bored with the cafe."

"Michelle, it's the time we like. Good. Michelle, when you wake up, you will have lost all your desire to work at the hot baths. You will never again want to work at the baths. Working at the baths would be a bad thing. I'm tapping the egg, wake up. Michelle, how do you feel?"

"Fine. As always. I have had an idea, though. I thought I might try and get a job at the hot baths."

CHAPTER FIVE

"ERNEST."

"Yes, Michelle."

They were proceeding gently along Broad Walk with the park on their right. It was early evening, after work. They intended to walk up Bath Road and have a quiet drink at the Sun Inn. Ernest would then see Michelle home to Silverlands.

"Ernest. You see, I thought I might give up the bedsit and get a proper flat. I can afford it. I'm getting very good money at the baths. The tips are really, really good, especially from the older men. And if I get this flat, you know, with more rooms and so on, I wondered..."

"You wondered?"

"I wondered if you might come and live in it with me."

"What? Live with you, Michelle? As a flatmate?"

"No, Ernest, not as a flatmate."

"As man and wife, you mean? But we don't...I mean, we haven't ever..."

She stopped in the middle of Broad Walk, turned to face him, held both his hands and said, in a loud and clear voice, "What? You mean we don't sleep with each other? Is that all you men ever think about?"

"Michelle! Please! No need to shout!"

Michelle giggled. "Sorry. Just having a joke."

"Well it's not a very funny one. People can hear you. In any case, my mother would go scatty. I can't come and live with you. One, it would be called living in sin, even if there wasn't any. Sin, I mean. And two, being under the same roof with you when we weren't actually sinning...I think it would be more than a human man could stand."

"If we were - actually. Would you live with me then?"

"If we were, actually, or if I ever thought we would, actually, I should want to marry you."

"You would ask me to marry you if we had been to bed?"

"If I ever thought you would be willing to, yes. It's all that stops me asking you. I do love you, Michelle. But living with you in wedlock and all that, and being rejected by you all the time, well, it would drive me mad. Surely you can see that. I mean, I can put up with it as we are. I mean, we're not supposed to do it anyway. But if we were married..."

They talked for another hour in The Sun but it was all circular. They were no further forward at the end of a repeating series of ifs and buts. Ernest could not understand it. His beloved Michelle, the beauty whom he adored and for whom he would die, could talk about the thing he wanted most in the world, and she could say she was just as keen as he was, but she would not or could not do anything about it. Would she ever change? How much longer could he carry on? Would he be able to love another, even if he wanted to? He went back to see Gitana. Maybe she could help.

He was not a little surprised to find Gitana in full regalia, as if for a ceremony in the temple. She had on a small crown, more than a tiara, a coronet but obviously of ancient design, and a necklace of mayoral proportions, a substantial, Cleopatra-ish affair of silver and gold and what looked to Ernest like a king's ransom in rubies and emeralds. Her robe was more of a cloak than a dress, with strange patterns woven into it in many colours.

"Oh, I'm sorry" said Ernest. "I'll come back later."

"Come in, Ernest. It's you I have been expecting. So. What about Aelius Motio?"

"What about him? What about me and Michelle?"

"In a moment. What have you discovered about Mister Motio?"

"All right. There was a Roman fort at Brough-on-Noe..."

"Where's that?"

"...near Castleton, Hope, that way, as I was about to say, and the fort was then called Navio. It stood on the main route from here to Manchester. Anyway, a kind of an altar was found there, which had a carved inscription on it that I couldn't understand, not the way it was quoted in the book in the library. It said 'Deae Arnomecte Ael Motio V S L L M'."

"It definitely said Motio."

"It definitely said Motio. What is this for?"

"Tell you later. Tell me about Motio."

"I went to see my old Latin master and he explained. The letters were an abbreviation, a convention, like we have RSVP on invitations. Everybody knew what they meant. It saved the stonemason having to carve the lot. He wrote it down for me. My Latin master, that is, not the stone mason. Here."

"Votum Solvit Laetus Libens Merito. Meaning, Ernestus?"

"They really should educate girls more. Latin instead of domestic science. Votum, a vow, Solvit, paid, Laetus Libens Merito, joyfully, freely, deservedly. So the whole inscription, if you put in the bits that are not actually there but are understood, means something like 'This altar is dedicated to the Goddess Arnomecta by Aelius Motio, a vow paid joyfully, freely and deservedly. He's saying that he has made and dedicated this altar, like he said he would, and he's delighted to do so."

"In return for some favour or other, presumably."

"Yes, that's it. Apparently you would go to the shrine of the goddess, ask her to cure your toothache or your wife's barrenness, and you would promise something in return. If it was a big favour, you promised something big, like an altar, which is what old Aelius Motio did. Satisfied? Now, what about me and Michelle? What's in the stars?"

"Ernest. Have you noticed something? Have you noticed that no astrologer ever writes out a forecast for himself on, say, his thirtieth birthday, to be read out in public on his fortieth? Why don't they do that?"

"I see. You're saying there's nothing in it and you're not going to look into my future."

"That's what I'm saying. I do it, I know, but that's just for the money. It's what people want. I know the techniques, I have the knowledge, I supply the need."

"This was part of your studies in the pagan university."

"If you will, Ernest, yes. Make some tea while I tell you about it. The thing is, it used to be considered a religious science and, in a way, it was. That was so in Iron Age Britain, when they believed in Arnemetia, and in all the other ancient civilisations. You had some very clever chaps, the priests, observing the heavens and gradually becoming able to predict the movements of stars. They could devise a precise calendar, tell when there would be an eclipse, and so on. If they could say what was going to happen Up There and when, it was only a short step to predicting what it all meant for the future Down Here. Which, then as now and provided you weren't too precise about your predictions, was a nice easy way to earn a good living."

"Did they believe it? The priests?"

"Possibly. I don't know."

"But you don't believe it, do you, Gitana?"

"No, Ernest, I don't."

"So you're not going to tell me if I'm going to marry Michelle."

"No. If I may continue? Along came the Greeks, who refined and expanded the system. You have to remember that the world was a small place then, and civilisation even smaller. It was easily imagined that gods and stars could be directly involved in your life, just as you could imagine that there was a heaven with enough room in it for everybody and that blood sacrifices went straight to the Olympian corridors of power."

"Did the Greeks do all that too?"

"They did, but science advances, Ernest. It eventually became obvious that sacrificing fatted calves and virgins did not do a lot for the public weal. Such aspects of the scientific canon were discredited. I think the Greeks were ahead of the Ancient British in that respect. Likewise, when it was eventually discovered that the earth revolves around the sun, that what goes up must come down and that there are eight sausages to the pound, astrology was discredited as a science."

"And yet, people still believe it. Not me, of course" Ernest hastened to add. "And what's in this tea? It tastes like hedge clippings."

"Ah, you've picked mine up by mistake. Here, swap. That's just a little extra something I popped in to help clear my mind. Makes a change from the lamb's blood."

"Lamb's blood?"

"Mine is a world full of nonsense but I do believe that certain people can see. I believe that the only way to prophesy anything worth a damn is to be born with extra perceptions and to express yourself while your ordinary senses are suspended. Ernest, I shall be leaving you shortly. Mentally, at any rate. My departure may result in a demonstration of what I have just told you. My extract of hedge clippings, as you call it, takes me away. I can reach the state of ecstasy rather more easily with that, than I can with the blood of the sacrificial victim. That's what the Greek oracles used to drink. Lamb's blood. Or bull's. I can feel myself slipping. Don't worry. Go and sit over there and don't do anything. It's beginning to work, and whatever happens from now on, don't mind. Just listen. Just listen. Just listen."

Gitana closed her eyes and sat back on the locker seat. Her breathing became steadier and her face, even with her eyes closed, seemed to be setting itself in a look of determination. After perhaps a minute like this, her hands went to her throat and undid her necklace.

Her hands fell to her sides and she stood up. As she stood, the necklace parted and her entire apparel stayed behind on the seat. Layers of various materials and colours, with cloak and undercloak and shift and skirt and petticoat, were all suspended somehow from each other and from the necklace. They all fell away at once, leaving her standing before Ernest, stark naked except for her coronet.

Had Ernest been able to anticipate this extremely startling revelation, he might have foreseen a jewel in the navel, perhaps, or an intricately contrived golden snake wound around each breast. As it was, this being the first time he had seen a naked woman, never mind one of such fine proportions, he saw nothing but her nakedness. Had she been tattoo'd with a scale map of the British Empire he probably would not have noticed.

Her eyes opened slowly and looked at Ernest, or rather into Ernest, and her arms spread and her fingers beckoned. When Ernest the slave got there, Gitana placed her hands one on each shoulder and held him at arm's length, still staring right through his pupils directly into his brain.

When Gitana's voice came, it was her own voice but changed, as if it had gone down an octave.

"You want love, and you seek it where there is none. You are under a spell which must be broken. You want love, and there is love, but it cannot be given from that place."

Gitana pulled Ernest to her and he felt the seer's naked bosom pushed against him. He could feel her heart beating at a terrific rate. Ernest was electrified suddenly to feel the other's pubis pushed hard against him, as a forward girl with hot intentions might while dancing cheek to cheek with a man who was slow on the uptake.

Gitana kissed Ernest on the neck and breathed softly in his ear. He imagined sweet nothings but instead heard a new version of the voice, a higher, purified variety. It was Gitana, but somehow it sounded like Michelle when hypnotised. Or it sounded like Michelle would sound, if Michelle were a boy soprano. This fine singing voice said an astonishing sentence. It said "There's nothing like killing someone to make you feel better."

Ernest, eyes and mouth wide open in shock, felt the soothsayer's grip loosen and watched her collapse slowly back into her seat. She was breathing more slowly, so slowly that Ernest thought she had stopped. She had died from the effort! When he leaned over to feel her heart - trying very hard not to feel her breasts at the same time but not quite succeeding - the pulse was there, powerful and steady. She looked as if she was asleep and would not wake for a long time, like someone who has had far too much to drink and has been put to bed, there to stay in deep unconsciousness until a normal balance in the blood stream is restored.

It seemed chilly in the caravan. Gitana's clothes were being sat on by their ex-wearer and Ernest could not pull them out from beneath the bare prophet. Ernest, honorable by nature, found a blanket, put it over sleeping beauty and wrote her a note.

'I want another session. Tomorrow, same time, unless I hear. Ernest.' As he was leaving he had the flash of a thought. This was a show! That's all it was, especially put on for him. Gitana was trying to pretend to be that goddess, Arnemetia. It was so much more jiggery pokery and mystical nonsense, staged because the fortune teller was out of her depth with the hypnosis. Or she fancied him, and wanted to get him away from Michelle...that was it! Seduction by magic! And he nearly fell for it! He turned back, banging his head on the porch bracket.

"Ow! Damn it! I was going to say, farewell to thee, Arnemetia, O mighty priestess of the spring waters and goddess of the grove. I wonder who the god was, who was in charge of killing people. To make you feel better, that is."

Ernest had often heard the expression 'to jump out of one's skin' but had not realised until that moment that such an athletic feat was very nearly possible. As his last light-hearted word faded into silence, Gitana sat bolt upright, her eyes wide open and blazing, the blanket falling away as her right hand shot out and her index finger pointed with vehement emphasis at the centre of the forehead of her transfixed subject, Ernest.

The seer's mouth opened wide and round, and words came from it without any movement of lips or tongue, as if she were nothing but a loudspeaker, a public-address horn relaying a message in a form a human could receive and understand.

The voice which came from the open mouth was the soprano version but very big, a hundred times bigger.

"Arnemetia is not mocked!" shouted the voice in enormous anger. "She brings destruction! It was men who took her from the world, and men shall be judged!"

The loudspeaking mouth closed and the human amplifier slept again. It took Ernest a minute or two to feel he was comfortably back in his skin and that Gitana was not going to make any more pronouncements from Hades. He forced himself to go near her to retrieve his note. He needed to think about this. The attractions of promised free love with a (slightly) older woman might be outweighed by the hellfire that seemed to go with it. He had the courage and the manners to rearrange the blanket - he could still feel the cold in that van, despite the warmth of summer outside - but that was it. He could not get out through that door fast enough.

Over the next few days he made several important decisions but each decision reversed the previous one. He decided to leave Michelle behind and move to Nottingham, where the ghost of D H Lawrence would surely inspire him to greatness. Then, he decided to marry Michelle. They would discover passion on their wedding night and never look back. A few hours later, he decided to have an affair with Gitana and allow Michelle to find out. This might energise her into a choice: marry him, or stay a spinster.

After sleeping on this one, he decided to go to London, get a job in a publisher's office and write a novel in his spare time about goddesses and fortune tellers. If Michelle truly loved him, she would give up her job at the baths and come to him in London. On the other hand, he could stay in Buxton with things as they were, and wait a little longer. He could be more patient. Give her time. What was that line from Andrew Marvell? 'But at my back I always hear, Time's winged chariot hurrying near.' Yes, that was it, wasn't it. Ode to his Coy Mistress. 'Had we but world enough, and time, This coyness, Lady, were no crime.' How right you are, Mr Marvell. 'The grave's a fine and private place, But none, I think, do there embrace.' Quite so. Or maybe he should move to Nottingham.

....

'Anonymous', 'boring', 'mundane', 'commonplace' and 'miserable bastard' were all words which had been used, some of them many times, to describe

Lucas C Stride III. During the war he had been a clerk in US Army supplies on a training base, where he acquired a reputation for precise rule-following to the point of obsession. Soldiers drawing from the stores knew there were two basic types of stores clerk. One didn't care a toss and was happy to deal for cash at the back door; the other viewed every item in the stores as his personal possession and was extremely reluctant to let anyone have anything unless compelled to do so by immaculate paperwork. Lucas C Stride III was indubitably in the latter grouping and was possibly its greatest exemplar in history.

Nobody liked Lucas. He sometimes wondered why he didn't have any friends. He sometimes wondered why women tried to get away from him as soon as they met him and avoided him, plague-like, thereafter. He put it down to lack of perceptiveness on the part of those particular members of the human race with whom he was unfortunate enough to deal.

His only sexual experience had been with a prostitute who, unknown to Lucas, had been paid by a whip-round among his work colleagues purely so that she could tell them all about it afterwards. She did, and she was quite upset by the whole occurrence, saying it was the worst of her professional life and likening it to being attacked by a herd of wet toads. She insisted on another five dollars to get drunk on, so she could forget the episode at least for a day.

Lucas' one release and source of pleasure was travel. He had been to every tourist attraction in his home State of Arkansas and in every surrounding State. He'd also been to Cuba and Mexico, and now here he was in England.

The trip had not turned out quite as expected. For example, a bumpy journey in the back of an old Morris van had not been on the itinerary. In fact, the entire fortnight's schedule featured travel by train only. Dinner that evening was being missed. He should have been in the highly rated restaurant of the Midland Hotel in Manchester, tasting the finest delights, instead of which he had had no dinner at all. He hadn't even had a drink, much less the Manhattan cocktail he had planned to be followed by a half bottle of something French, possibly a Montrachet or a Mouton Cadet. He would have taken the sommellier's advice on that one, which again depended on the waiter's advice on what to have for his main course. He did like steak but he didn't think the English would know much about steaks. In any case, in a French restaurant, as he believed the Midland's to be, he would clearly want to eat à la Français.

After his two days in Manchester, following his two days in Buxton, he was to travel first class - he never stinted himself on holiday since it was the only time of year he spent any money - to London Euston. He would send his luggage on to the Strand Palace Hotel but would travel himself by the London subway, or 'tube' as he knew they called it.

After that there would be theatres, galleries - he was quite a cultured man, despite his social ineptness - and restaurants. Possibly he might even go to the Windmill Theatre, if he felt courageous enough.

That these moments of pleasure failed to materialise was a mere bagatelle, a string of minor inconveniences, compared to the really big thing that had gone wrong for Lucas C Stride III. The really big thing was that he was now dead, murdered, and was in a sack in the back of an old van, on his way to his last resting place instead of a warm and comfortable billet in the sumptuous Midland Hotel.

"Drive to Glossop, then turn along the Snake Pass towards Sheffield" said Michelle.

"Do you think that will be far enough away?"

"More than far enough, Ernest. I know exactly where we want to be. At least, I will when we get there."

"You do? You will? How come? You've never been up those hills."

"Get on with it, Ernest. Glossop, and turn right."

It was a filthy night, blowing a gale and pouring with that especially penetrating kind of cold rain so often a feature of British upland regions. The van's windscreen wiper singularly failed to cope and Ernest drove very slowly and very carefully, protecting the old van as much as he could against the steeps and windings of the Snake Pass. What small amount of other traffic they saw was doing the same and visibility beyond the headlights was absolutely nil.

"This is it. Here. This is the place."

"Michelle, it's just another bit of wet hillside. Why is it so special?"

"I don't know. It just is. Now, are you going to help me or not?"

Ernest was able to pull the van off the road a little. Anyone going past now, if they noticed it at all, would assume that someone had decided enough was enough and was sleeping the worst of the weather away.

"Give me the spade. We'll pick the spot before we bring him" said Michelle. "Come on, Ernest, do come on! Now, you see here, this is where the proper road from Buxton to Manchester goes. The new road veers off to the left, see, but the real road goes straight on. Come along, it will be good walking. We only need to make a few yards and we'll find some really boggy ground."

Ernest had no idea what she was talking about but was already resolved to do what she said without question. She shone her torch around as she walked and, after quite some time, found what she was looking for. Her 'few yards' were more like a mile, Ernest thought, but at least it meant they were so far into the bog that poor old whojer-maflip would never be found.

"There!" announced Michelle. "I'll start digging. You go back and get him. He's not very heavy."

And so they buried Lucas C Stride III, one of the first American tourists to come to Buxton since the war and the last Lucas C Stride, since he was a single man with no relatives - well, none who cared a jot about him anyway.

The journey home to Michelle's new flat tested Ernest's driving skills and the van's capabilities to the utmost. The conditions were atrocious but they got there. By the time Michelle had run a bath, Ernest was asleep on the settee with his coat drying by the fire and the rest of his clothes still on. She smiled when she looked at him. Everything would be all right now. Soon they could be happy. Stride with his sly, slimy fingers was rotting in the ground, revenge had been exacted and she could prepare herself for Ernest. She would buy a new nightdress. She would go and look at nightdresses in the shops. A negligee, it would be, of floaty material you could almost see through. She would buy one and put it in the wardrobe, and when the time was right Michelle Mercer and Ernest Mycock would be one. Soon. It would be soon. She went to her bath.

Ernest slept late and awoke to realise that he had been out all night for the first time. He didn't particularly want to face his mother until he had a really plausible story to tell in convincing detail. Making up such a story was all the more difficult because his mother's obvious assumption - that he would be lying to cover up sleeping with Michelle - was far from the truth. The truth was a lot worse, while his mother would probably smile knowingly and say something awful about making an honest woman of Michelle.

He asked Michelle to call in at the office where he worked, on her way to the baths, with a message to say he was feeling poorly but hoped to be in later. He would wait until he knew his mother would be out at the market, go home and get changed. He didn't tell Michelle that he was also going to do some geographical research.

Home and in something of a daze, he ferreted among his old papers to find an Ordnance Survey map of the area and tried to work out exactly where they had been the previous night in the rain. They'd crossed the high point of the Pass, he knew, if only because the little van had been so grateful for a bit of downhill running, but they hadn't quite got as far as the Snake Inn, he was fairly certain of that...good heavens above! He looked, and looked again. There it was. 'ROMAN ROAD (course of)' it said. 'Doctor's Gate' it said. Time for a visit to the library.

In a book with a map of Roman Britain, sure enough, the route of Doctor's Gate was marked. A lesser road from Buxton to Manchester, that is Aquae Arnemetiae to Mancunium, appeared to follow the same way as the modern road along the side of the Goyt valley to Whaley Bridge and on, but the major Roman route to Manchester and the north west did something quite different. It set off north east, before veering sharply west along what they now called Snake Pass.

He looked at more maps. Here was the Roman road from Buxton, called Batham Gate, heading off through Peak Dale and Peak Forest, then Bradwell to Brough-on-Noe, site of the Roman fort called Navio and the famous altar by A Motio. There it took a ninety degree turn, heading for the Snake which it met where the River Alport flows into the Ashop. The Romans then followed the contour higher up the hillside, above the Snake until Dinas Sitch Tor where the routes became the same for the climb up Lady Clough. Then, at Doctor's Gate, soon after the Snake Inn going west, they parted. The modern Snake Pass went its own, newer way to Glossop and the Romans chose Doctor's Gate. The Romans. Presumably they'd followed an even older track or trading route. Theirs was the proper road.

He went back home, intending to have a cup of tea and a sandwich before heading for the office, but there was a note on the mat. 'Please come to the caravan as soon as you can. Gitana'.

Ernest hadn't seen Gitana since the naked trance and now arrived at her door to find her looking sad, anguished, disappointed, angry, all at the same time. This was how you might look, Ernest thought, if the doctor had called you in to say you had three months to live. It seemed obvious to him that, somehow, by supernatural powers, whatever, somehow, she knew.

"Where have you put the American?" she said.

Ernest sat down. It was his turn to look as if he had three months to live.

"It's beyond my strength, Gitana, all of this. She made me borrow Alsop's van. It's only a Morris Eight and goodness knows how old it is. It's all right for a few light deliveries on a sunny afternoon but it's not meant for carrying three people and various tools over the Snake Pass, head on into a gale and a thunderstorm. How did you know, anyway?"

"I know. And this will not be the last."

"Nonsense. That's the whole idea. She's purged of this thing, whatever it is. She's kind of purified. She's sacked her demons. We buried them with the American at Doctor's Gate."

"I'm afraid not, Ernest. This is the beginning, not the end. Unless we do something to stop her, there will be more."

"Look, Gitana, I know you're very good at this, but I insist there will be no more. This is a one-off. I am convinced of it. Michelle wants to get married and live happily ever after. We shall soon forget the American. I am sorry for him and his family, but if it had to be Michelle or him, I'm going for Michelle."

"What exactly is the Doctor's Gate?"

"It's a Roman road. It's a section of the old route. The Snake Pass now leaves it and goes in a loop while the Roman road goes straight on towards Glossop. They say that some doctor years ago used to use it so it got its modern name from him, but I don't know if that's true."

"And why did you go there, to bury the American?"

"She wanted to."

"She?"

"Michelle, of course. She said she would know the right place when she saw it."

"Has Michelle become a student of ancient byways and burial grounds recently, or is it an old hobby of hers?"

"Well, yes, all right, Gitana, it was odd. I didn't understand it at the time and I still don't. But that doesn't prove there are going to be more...er, more, Americans."

"What it proves is, there is something working here that we don't know about. And that something will not be satisfied with one American, I promise you."

Ernest said nothing. He stared at the backs of his hands, hating the next moment when he would have to hear what Gitana was going to say.

"You said Michelle wants to get married. Do you, Ernest? Do you want to get married? How many Americans can you forgive, Ernest? If you can forgive this one, could you allow another? Or would three be the limit? Ernest? Two, or three?"

CHAPTER SIX

"MICHELLE! Is this you? Answer me!"

Ernest thumped his index finger into the front page of the Advertiser as the girl, seated in her own parlour, refused to look. She had on her hat and coat, ready to go to work where, in fact, she would be now if she hadn't been intercepted at her own front door by a raving lunatic waving the local paper.

"You've got no right coming in here like this, Ernest Mycock. Who do you think you are? Get out of my house this minute!"

"Mystery disappearance baffles police" read Ernest from the paper. "Mr Wadham Arnold Kelly, 53, of Leominster, Herefordshire, is recorded as entering the Hot Baths at Buxton last Wednesday morning for treatment. He is not recorded as leaving, despite a meticulously kept register of all comings and goings. His clothes and belongings, as well as himself, are inexplicably missing. None of the Hot Baths' staff can remember him being there after the first half hour of his appointment and no-one saw him depart. The police at Buxton received an enquiry from Mrs Kelly, who was expecting her husband home, etc etc. Have you done it again, Michelle? Have you?"

"Just leave me alone, Ernest. It's got nothing to do with you."

"Nothing to...who was it who carried your first one to his grave? Accessory after the fact, they call that. It's the same as if I'd done it myself. Nothing to do with me? Like hell it's nothing to do with me!"

"Oh, well, if that's all you're bothered about, don't you worry. I'm not going to tell on you. You won't be an accessory after the fact, before the fact or anywhere near the bloody fact, Ernest Mycock. So get back to your gypsy girlfriend and tell her. I won't be the one to drop you in it. In any case, it won't come to that."

"She's not my girlfriend. Look. You got away with the first one because nobody noticed he'd gone. It was pure luck. But the police are on to this. They might call in Scotland Yard!"

"Don't be stupid, Ernest. You are an idiot. Now, get back to your little clerk's desk and start scribbling. That's all you're good for."

"Michelle. This has to stop. It was a once-only thing, you said. And now you're expecting me and Gitana to stand by while you go around drowning innocent people."

"I didn't drown him. He'd been at the baths four days running. He kept making remarks."

"Making remarks? Making remarks? What? There should be a notice in the baths. Persons taking treatment are advised not to make remarks or they may find themselves put to death by drowning."

"I told you. I didn't drown him. If you really want to know, I put a rabbit snare around his neck and pulled it tight, then I made it tighter by twisting a stick. Then I held him under the water. That was after I'd done him with the snare. The water was after, so I didn't drown him. Then, when I put him in the sack, I hit him with a hammer. He'd been pinching my bottom. He tried to touch me."

"Jesus wept, Michelle. How did you get rid of him?"

"Same as always."

"Always? Same as always?"

"Same as we did, I mean. Before. With the American. I go to Mr Alsop and tell him you want to borrow the van. He gives me the key. I say you'll be along later to pick it up. When it's dark I go and get the van. I put the man in it. I drive it to the place, do the work, then I drive back and leave the van outside Alsop's shop. I put the key through the letterbox in an envelope with half a crown. You see? No link to you. And Alsop would never want to say anything."

"Michelle. Christ Almighty. You can't drive. You've never learned to drive. And what do you mean 'he gives me the key, I go and get the van, I put the man in it'? Is this some sort of a routine? 'I put the key through the letterbox'? How many times have you given Mr Alsop a half crown? What happens when I bump into him and he says something and I don't know what he's on about? How many times, Michelle? Ten bob's worth? A pound? A fiver?"

"Don't be silly, Ernest. Anyway, driving isn't so difficult. I've watched you do it. It's easy. I admit I'm not all that good at changing down. I can't do that double declutch thing like you. But the rest is perfectly all right, so I don't need you and I don't want you. I can keep you right out of it. You wouldn't want to be an accessory to Mr Kelly as well as the American, would you? Course not."

"I cannot believe I'm hearing this, Michelle. You make it sound like a bit of a prank, like something any girl might get up to. Come on, Doris, let's go, I've got the van, did you get the rabbit snares and the hammer? Good Lord above! And you're so cool and calm. You don't care, do you? I mean to say, after you've strangled somebody, soaked him for an hour or two, put him in a sack and staved his head in, you drive the dead body about the countryside in a semi-stolen van with no licence or insurance. Good God, next thing you'll be going down to Shufflebotham's and stealing your snares. How can I thank you for keeping me out of it like this?"

"Ernest. Please do not be such a cretin. You need not concern yourself about the police. You are not involved in any crime, because no crime has occurred as far as you are concerned. Even if it had, what have you to worry about? You're just an ex boyfriend. Now, go away and don't come back."

Ernest did what he always did these days when he needed help for his heart and mind. He went to Gitana.

"Yes, I've seen the paper, Ernest. I shall resist the temptation to say I told you so, in favour of what on earth are we going to do about it?"

"I was hoping you would tell me that. Can't you see how it's going to end?"

"I can't see anything clearly, and the gods know how I've tried. There's something in the way, something interfering, as if I'm trying to listen to the wireless in an attic while a foreign power is jamming the signal. So, all I've got is the ordinary equipment - a strictly limited quantity of intelligence, common sense and knowledge of the human race. You've got the same. What do you think?"

"I think we can't let this go on, Gitana. That's what I think. You know this latest one, this Mr Kelly, isn't the only one since the American?"

"Yes, I think I knew. In any case I'm not surprised. I told you...sorry. No, I'm not at all surprised."

"I can't say I care enormously about a few dirty old men getting their come-uppance, but that's not entirely the point, is it? I mean, she's murdering them, with her own bare hands. And she makes jolly sure they're dead, too. You know what she used on Kelly? A rabbit snare, like a garrotte, you know, twisted with a stick. Then she stuck his head under the water, then she bashed his skull in with a hammer. I mean, this is Michelle Mercer of Buxton Spa, Michelle of the fair and gentle sex, aged eighteen, not Bill Sikes crossed with Jack the Ripper."

"The threefold death."

"What?"

"Nothing. So, Ernest, applying the aforementioned normal equipment, the result is clear. We have a simple choice. Shop her, or stop her."

"Not shop her. I won't be a party to that. She still means...I mean, she was the first girl I..."

"Quite so. In which case, we have to devise a method of stopping her. Short of kidnapping her and locking her up, I can't see a lot in the way of strategies at the moment."

"If only we could get her away from those baths. The opportunity wouldn't arise after that, would it? You wouldn't get the dirty old men in an ordinary job."

"You get dirty old men everywhere, Ernest, but you are right. That is the first essential, get her away from the baths. Then all we have to do is brainwash her and find her a nice young man with whom she can settle down and have four children."

"You make it seem so easy."

"There is another option."

"Come on, then. What is it?"

"Kill her."

Ernest said nothing. He couldn't.

"Don't you see, Ernest? She will carry on murdering these men. I think there is a point where she will stop, when she's had her revenge, but I don't know where that point is or if she will reach it in this life. She is possessed, Ernest. She isn't Michelle Mercer any more."

"You sound like somebody in Dracula. Possessed? What are you talking about? Are you saying we've got to pierce her heart with a wooden stake at midnight or something? What is all this, Gitana? What rubbish are you talking?"

"It's not rubbish. You didn't hear all those hypnosis sessions. She was born for this, this mayhem and vengeance. It was her purpose."

"How do I know you didn't put this madness into her? How do I know the hypnosis didn't change her? I'm sorry, Gitana, but I'm not having any more of this ridiculous nonsense. Kill her! Kill Michelle? For the sake of a few middle-aged perverts? It's you who's mad. Goodbye!"

Ernest, in tears of rage and bewilderment, set off across the fields, heading for the Ashbourne road. In fifteen minutes he was walking down Terrace Road, towards the baths. Funnily enough, he'd never been in the baths before.

"Can I help you, sir?" enquired the receptionist.

Ernest quickly looked at the posted lists of treatments. 'Russian Bath' seemed to leap out at him.

"Yes, thank you" he said. "I wonder if I could have a Russian Bath?"

"Certainly. I'm sure the steam room is free at the moment. Would you like it with or without the cold showers?"

"Oh, er, with, I think. Yes, with."

In a few moments, Ernest was lying on a stone slab in a very small room full of steam, while a short and wiry man massaged his back.

"This is to promote the perspiration, sir. Must promote the actual perspiration of the pores, if you are to benefit fully."

Ernest didn't especially like being massaged by such a creepy little fellow but had to put up with it. Ten minutes of that and Ernest was sweating as he had never sweated before.

"Now, sir" said the attendant creep, who didn't seem to be affected by the steam heat at all, "keep that towel around you and I'll show you where the cold shower is. Have a cold shower, sir, icy cold it is. Don't you go staying in too long, just my little joke sir, and then come back here and lie on the slab for another ten, then you'll have another shower, and that's it. You won't be needing me any more. Thank you, sir. I hope you enjoy the rest of your treatment."

The shower was indeed icy. Ernest was surprised that water could be so cold and yet remain liquid. A minute was all he could stand and he was glad to be back on his slab, letting the steam bring his body back to its normal, blood-warm, non-shivering state.

When he heard the door go he imagined it must be Mr Creep coming back to make sure he'd been in the shower, but it wasn't Mr Creep. Mr Creep, Ernest felt sure, would not be dangling a braided copper wire noose in front of his eyes while holding something very sharply pointed to his neck.

"It would be messy, I know" said Michelle, "and I would be found out. But, on the other hand, you would be dead. So, are you going to listen? Are you?"

She moved the knife point a little, just enough to make him certain of her intentions. Ernest could not nod but he did manage a sort of 'yes'.

"Good. Now, Ernest, I know what you and Gitana are up to. I know you will try and stop me but, you see, you cannot. This is your one and only warning, for old times' sake. I think probably it is more warning than you and your gypsy girlfriend would give me. You see, Ernest, I loved you. I did. I loved you. But you are like all men. You cannot be trusted, and you have no patience. I must go. I shall get the sack if they find me here, and that would never do, would it? I should have to move to Matlock. Goodbye, Ernest. And don't go playing with matches."

Ernest was under the cold shower, dried, dressed and outside in rather less than the proverbial two shakes, and he ran most of the way back to Gitana's caravan. She gave him a special herbal tea to calm him down.

"What did she mean by me not playing with matches, Gitana?"

"I imagine she intends to fire the caravan with your gypsy girlfriend in it. Jealousy is a very powerful motivator, even when unjustified. She probably sees it as some kind of justice, you know, the priestess sacrificed in the flames instead of the virgin."

"Then you've got to get out. Come and stay at mother's. We've got a spare bedroom."

"I don't think so, thank you, Ernest. Michelle may believe she is on a holy crusade with divine rights, but there is no possibility of her getting anywhere near this caravan without me knowing. Don't worry about it. I told you. She is possessed, but that doesn't give her any special capabilities. She's still human, not superhuman. Or supernatural. More tea?"

Meanwhile, back at the baths, Mr Creep, or Mr Pearl as he was more properly known, was waiting for his next appointment to turn up. It was a Plombiere Douche. Mr Pearl liked giving Plombiere Douches, which was just a posh name for an enema given with spa water. It somehow suited Mr Pearl's sense of humour. His only regret was that the Ladies' and Gentlemen's sides of the hot baths were so rigorously kept. He would have liked giving Plombiere Douches to some of those fat old cows who treated girls like Michelle so arrogantly. They must think they're duchesses, those old cows, or douche-esses, just his little joke, and Michelle they looked down their noses at, as if she were an inferior life form about the equivalent of a mop and bucket.

Mr Pearl had a soft spot for Michelle. He was a secret admirer. He knew he could never be anything else, just as well as he knew every other little thing that went on in those baths. Nothing went by Mr Pearl, but Mr Pearl had no illusions. Knowledge might be power, but it wasn't a power he was likely to use in this case. He enjoyed his knowledge and that was all. Michelle would never look at him as a beau, and he wasn't going to pay for it like those others did. Not because he didn't want to, or he couldn't afford it. He would love it. He would spend every penny he had on it. Except he had a very good idea of what happened to them afterwards. They were never seen again. He didn't know exactly what she did with them and he didn't want to. Although his desire for Michelle burned with a pure white heat, it wasn't worth suffering the fate of the male spider. One swift mating and you're eaten. No, thank you. He would submerge his desires in silence. Where was his Plombiere Douche? He thought he would have a look in the entrance hall. Perhaps the customer was waiting there, not knowing the procedure.

Mr Pearl's hand stayed on the handle as he opened the door a crack and heard voices. Michelle was behind the desk, as she sometimes was when she filled in for the regular woman, and she was talking to a man, a rather portly, well dressed gentleman of obvious means. She was fixing a time! So, here was another spider being lured to his fate. It was no wonder that Michelle could afford her nice little house that she'd just moved in to. She must take a fortune off these men, that is, assuming she emptied their wallets before getting rid of them, however she did it. Mr Pearl counted one a fortnight for the last three months. This was the sixth. Mr Pearl could understand how they would fall for it. The prospect of spending an evening in a bed with Michelle would be enough to loosen any man's grip on his money. Well, well, well, so tonight's victim was this afternoon's Plombiere Douche. He was heading this way. Mr Pearl would ensure he got a very thorough douche indeed. After all, it would be his last.

Or, perhaps not. Plots were being laid in a gypsy caravan. Ever since

Michelle had her first hypnotic session, Gitana had been severely disturbed, partly by the events and partly by the revelation of previously underestimated powers in herself. She had been a student of mumbo jumbo and allowed herself a cautious acceptance of a faint possibility that there was something in it. Now she found that her feelings and her predictions kept coming true with awful regularity.

Just at this moment she was terribly confused. She and Ernest knew, logically, that the only thing to do was to point the authorities in Michelle's direction. They could do it anonymously. There would be no danger to themselves. The authorities would lock Michelle in the asylum and she could dream her life away in groves and gardens, kept well apart from any middle-aged men who might make remarks. This was obviously the sensible thing to do. Gitana hadn't meant the killing option seriously. It was only said to make Ernest realise how restricted their choices were.

The thing was agreed. The editor of the Buxton Advertiser would receive an anonymous and untraceable message, saying that the fate of Mr Kelly was known in the hot baths by one of the better looking female staff, a dark-haired girl aged only eighteen.

Despite their agreement, and despite the unarguable rightness of the action, and despite the complete lack of any alternatives, Gitana felt it was wrong. She wasn't certain if it was wrong in itself or if it would go wrong, rebound somehow for the worse, but she knew...what? She knew something, but couldn't say what it was. She asked Ernest for a few days to sort out her thoughts. They agreed a maximum of three. Three days from now, the editor would have his message unless Gitana came up with another solution to the problem which, she admitted, was most unlikely. Ernest went home with a heavy but restful heart. He knew the whole dreadful business was over. He could start getting on with the rest of his life.

At exactly half past seven that evening, the portly, well dressed Plombiere Douche knocked on the door of a small but well set house in the Silverlands district. He was a bit of a scholar, this chap, and made it his business to find out about the history of places he visited. Silverlands, he knew, having looked up a few things about Buxton, was where the original Roman settlement had been. He speculated that it was called Silver, not after the metal but after the Latin word Silva, silvae, meaning woods.

The door opened, the man raised his hat, and in he went. Inside the little house everything was neatly arranged and of sound quality. It was a comfortable private home, not rich or gaudy but sensible. In the front parlour, a gas fire made its rushing noise and there was an armchair and a settee with velvet cushions. The gentleman was shown to the armchair and offered a choice of tea, whisky or French wine. He chose whisky, with a little water if you please.

When the whisky came, the gentleman offered to pay the agreed fee in advance, but that was not necessary. After all, he might be so pleased with the service that he would want to increase the fee! Now, this was how things would go. First, there would be a change of clothes for the young woman, from the current dressing gown to something more interesting. Then, there would be a dance. This would be performed by the light of the standard lamp, which stood in the bay window. So long as the dancer stayed this side of the lamp, there would be no inflammatory or seductive silhouettes on the curtains. The gas fire would have to be turned off, but the dance would make sure the gentleman was warm enough. The gentleman in question stirred in his chair at the thought of inflammatory or seductive silhouettes.

When the dance was finished, the gentleman could have another anticipatory whisky with the dancer on his knee, or they could go upstairs to the bedroom straightaway. How did that sound? The gentleman, examining the schedule in his mind, was more than happy to concede that it sounded most attractive. Let the dance begin!

The dancer went from the room and returned a short time later dressed in an arrangement of what looked like long coloured chiffon scarves. She hummed to herself as she swayed too and fro, waving her arms in an oriental manner. With a slow spinning movement she arrived at the gentleman's side and offered him the end of a scarf to hold. He held it, and stirred in his seat again as the dancer spun away from him, leaving the scarf, or veil as he realised he must now call it, to lie where it fell.

The dancer repeated this movement, with variations, five more times, with enticing intervals between. Now she was dressed only in one long veil, which covered her hips and upper body but did not conceal their features. The gentleman offered no resistance as the dancer knelt before him and tied his hands together with the end of this long last veil. His eyes were wide. He could almost feel the softness of the skin on the breasts which were half exposed to him. Now she stood and spun away from him and the veil peeled from her breasts and he saw the whole of them and was deprived of all ability to move. She continued her circles, gradually shifting out of his line of sight. Obviously, she would continue around the back of the armchair and present herself to him, finally, completely naked. On the way, she stayed for a moment directly behind him.   Part of the veil was being dangled in front of his eyes. It was the other end! She must be naked now. His hands were tied at one extreme of the last veil and here was the other! The dancer's hand waved the airy, insubstantial material in front of his face. It was the final tease. They both knew she was nude but agreed to maintain the secret a little longer. The dancer's hand brushed the man's lips with the veil and then slipped a part of it between them. He felt her tie it behind his head. How delicious! When he saw her, when she showed herself to him with nothing hidden, he would be silkily bound and gagged by the last veil, the one which so lately had lain against her skin, which had kissed the surfaces of those magnificent breasts and swathed those lusciously swaying young hips! The man could not help himself giving a tiny groan of longing. Any second now and she would appear in front of his eyes, a naked goddess. He could hardly bear the thought of it. Oh, there would be no question of her sitting on his knee. If he didn't get her upstairs soon, it would be too late. He had not been so excited for years. Come, goddess, come into view! Now!

    He wondered for a fraction of a second what was that wire which passed before his eyes and then he wondered no longer as he fought for his life. He kicked and wriggled and heaved. He almost succeeded in overturning the armchair but then realised he was wrong to try. He should welcome the shadows in his eyes and the tranquility they promised. Someone must have turned the gas fire back on. He could hear its rushing sound, quite loudly, disturbing the peace. Through a mist he could see a tall, very well made young woman, stripped bare of all her clothes. She was carrying a heavy iron poker with a brass handle. She was carrying it by the point, with the handle towards him. Why, he thought, did she need a poker, when she had a gas...

CHAPTER SEVEN

TWO glum men sat in a pub in Glossop.
"What a bastard" said one, taking a long pull on his pint.
"What a bastard" said the other, putting his Park Drive out with unusual force.

These men were dressed in army boots and heavy outdoor clothes - knee breeches, thick khaki stockings, light blue shirts of heavy cotton, Fair Isle wool jumpers, tweed jackets. Beside them on the pub floor were two blue canvas rucksacks, the kind with a metal frame. The rucksacks were bulging with their contents and looked as if they must weigh a great deal. Tin cups and billy cans hung from straps and buckles and a bedroll was fastened across the top of each. Anyone seeing such preparations would have realised that here were two men on serious business. Perhaps they were off to discover the North West Passage and had stopped in Glossop for a quick pint on the way. Possibly they were stragglers from an Everest expedition which had strayed into Derbyshire or, more likely, they were out to find the famous and mysterious man-eating Mam Tor Monster.

In fact, for them, the expedition was over. They had been talking about it for ten years and more, before and all through their war service as RAF mechanics, and planning it in detail for a whole twelve months. They had, they thought, foreseen everything. Obviously, they had not and they were finished almost before they had begun.

In June 1935, a keen rambler called Tom Stephenson had published an article in a magazine suggesting a long-distance footpath, the Pennine Way. It would be 30 years before his idea became a reality but there was a proposed route which had been surveyed in 1939 and the Dower Report on National Parks in 1945 recommended that the Pennine Way should be laid out and agreed as soon as possible. For these two men of Manchester, Eric Chalmers and Colin Banham, this meant that the thing they'd talked about whenever they'd met, ever since they'd read Stephenson's article, was as good as done. If Eric and Colin could now walk the surveyed route, from Edale in

Derbyshire to Kirk Yetholm in Berwickshire, they would be the first people ever to do it.

The fly in their Fiery Jack ointment was the very reason why it would take so many more years before the Pennine Way could be declared open. Those sections of the walk, totalling 180 miles, which went along established rights of way were joined together by 70 more miles of bits and pieces with no legal access. These parts went across land which its owners currently saw as private, but Eric and Colin were not the sort to worry about a bit of trespassing. They were good navigators and hardy. If things looked dodgy, if there were farmers and landowners about with shot guns, they would walk at night.

They began their planning early in 1946, intending to make the journey the following year. Looking at the map, their first problem would occur within a couple of hours of setting out. Leaving Edale there was a public footpath up Grinds Brook but over the top of Kinder Scout there was nothing. Kinder Scout was, they knew, a flat topped giant bog, cut everywhere with peat groughs, some very deep and most with water and sticky, leg-holding slop in the bottom. Kinder Scout was a horrible place to get lost. In mist and rain you could go around in circles. In mist and rain at night, trespassing, you might be separated from your colleague and stuck to your waist in wet peat, and that would be that.

As it happened, when they went up there, the night was clear and the moon was shining. They left Edale before dark, so they just had the top crossing to do blind, as far as Kinder Downfall, when they met up with a footpath again and became legal. After that they walked on until dawn, found a secluded spot a mile or so short of the top of Mill Hill and pitched the tent. They slept until mid-morning. If any irate grouse-moor owner had come by, it would have looked as if they had come up the public path through William Clough.

The sun was quite hot by the time they'd had their breakfast, struck camp and got on their way. There was an old path here too, although strictly speaking the Pennine Way didn't follow it closely, but still they felt it was near enough to be done by day. They walked over the road which was the Snake Pass at its summit and, half a mile further on, crossed Doctor's Gate.

"Pass the binocs, Eric" said Colin. "I just want to have a look at...bleeding bloody hell. It's an arm!"

The burial party had apparently taken no trouble to strip the body of its identity. His passport was in his inside pocket and so the police had no trouble at all in concluding that the arm and, indeed, the rest of the remains, freshly preserved in the acid peat, belonged to Lucas C Stride III, the last of the Lucas Strides. Two days later they were highly puzzled by the pathologist's report. It said that death was caused by drowning, whereas first sight of the body had rather suggested that the large hole in the back of his head might have had something to do with it. This wound, the pathologist decided, was made after death, with a blunt instrument, possibly the ball of a hammer. Similarly, the bruises and cuts on the neck were made after the drowning. They were caused by a tightened ligature, possibly a piece of braided wire such as that used for rabbit snares.

The trail was a little cool - it was three months since the unremarkable Mr Stride had disappeared without anyone noticing - but dogged detective work revealed his last known movements. Thank goodness he had been American or the job would have much more difficult. He had arrived in Buxton, at the Portland Hotel, with little luggage, just a couple of small cases, saying that he had had most of it sent from Liverpool to the Midland Hotel in Manchester, where he was booked to stay for two days after two days in Buxton, sampling the waters. A telephone call to the Midland confirmed that they still had several trunks and cases consigned to them by the shipping line and could the police please tell them what to do with them?

Mr Stride had paid his bill at the Portland on the second morning and left his baggage at the desk, asking the girl to have it sent on to the station. The hotel did not expect to see him again and so thought no more about him.

At the station, a search of left luggage revealed two small cases with no labels and no records. They must have been taken in to the office because there was nothing better to do with them. When opened, they proved to contain men's clothes including suspenders for socks and several bow ties, which seemed American enough to the Derbyshire Constabulary, plus a copy of The New Yorker magazine, some traveller's cheques in sterling and some in US dollars, and a diary.

The last entry in the diary read as follows:

Buxton water seems like regular water. Tastes of nothing. Don't see how it can cure arthritis or any other damned thing. Much better for me would be a round or two with one of the girls at the Baths. She is stupendous. Reminds me of that new movie actress, Ava Gardner. Must see if I can get a date tomorrow!

The detective inspector in charge of the case read this entry with great interest and asked if there were any film fans in the team. Who was 'that new movie actress, Ava Gardner'? What did she look like? A rather embarrassed WPC admitted to going to the pictures at least twice a week and sometimes on Sundays as well. She had seen The Killers, in which the femme fatale was played by this beautiful, dark haired young woman with green eyes and a very fine, er, figure, sir. Did the WPC mean that Miss Gardner had a large bosom? Indeed so, sir. Right. All they had to do was find a girl who worked at the baths who had dark hair, possibly green eyes, was good looking and had an enviable chest. Get to it, lads.

There was a light knock on the cell door. A gentle tap rather than the usual barging in had become the habit of the Holloway prison warders ever since the first few days, when they discovered that Miss Mercer, multiple murderess, was really Miss Mercer from another world. The warders found her frightening, really, as a junior dresser or call boy might find one of the grande dames of the theatre. While there was nothing grand about Miss Mercer's behaviour, there was certainly a distance and an almost regal self-possession. The warders imagined St Joan being tied to the stake or St Catherine to her wheel. Those doing the tying would know that they were in the presence of a person quite unlike themselves, a person who would not be touched by whatever sufferings or indignities were forced upon her. They could burn the body but the flames could not scorch the impeccable soul. They could break the bones but the spirit was adamant, without scar or scratch.

"Come in" said Michelle, possibly the first prisoner to have had this well mannered relationship with a gaol's keepers since the gaol was the Tower and the prisoner a high born and wealthy Ladyship.

The warder found the girl reading a very large and forbidding-looking book.

"What are you reading?" she inquired, wondering at the girl's calmness. There was, after all, less than twenty four hours to go.

"Confucius" said Michelle. "Chinese philosopher. Never to late to learn, eh? What do you say?"

"Yes, I'm sure. I'm not one for books much. I prefer the pictures."

"I was like that. I preferred the pictures. Errol Flynn, Douglas Fairbanks, Laurence Olivier. I can't get out to see them so much now, so I read books instead."

"The Marx Brothers I like. I like a good laugh...er, look, Michelle, Miss Mercer, it's customary, as it were, ah, in these circumstances, you see, to ask the, er, the person, that is to say, if she wants, if there is anything..."

"Any last requests, you mean? Of course. Mine is very simple. I should like a half pint glass of Buxton spring water."

"Is that all? A glass of water?"

"Buxton water. A glass of Buxton water. From the warm spring. I don't want cigarettes or caviar, or fillet steak or whisky. Thank you."

Michelle returned to her Confucius as the warder went off in some puzzlement. Confucius was philosophising about springs. The well from which water is drawn conveys the idea of an inexhaustible dispensing of nourishment, he was saying. The spring symbolises the most basic needs of mankind. Whatever else happens and whatever other circumstances mankind brings about, his needs remain eternally the same and this cannot be changed. Life has no end and its foundations are the same in everyone. Everyone has an element of the divine in his nature and just as he draws water from the well, so he can draw spiritual nourishment from his divinity.

The young woman thought these ancient words, written two and a half thousand years before, made a tremendous amount of good sense. Her own words uttered only minutes ago, those forming her last request, were provoking much lively argument among the warders and their supervisors, not all of whom were drawing on their divine side. The governor himself was brought into it. To get Buxton water, someone would have to get on the train, go to Buxton with a bottle, collect it and come back. Such a thing was possible in the time but, suggested the governor, a man of great experience but who had not yet met Miss Mercer, was it worth it? Why not just give her a glass of London tap water and tell her it was from Buxton? She'd never know.

Some of the others in the discussion were against that idea. Possibly Buxton water tasted peculiar or even horrible, like some spa waters do.

Another warder, who thought her sister had been to Buxton once before the war, had a vague memory that Buxton water was just like ordinary water, tasteless, except it came out warm. Several of the debaters made the point that, even if she would never know, that was not the issue. It was her last request. They were going to hang her by the neck until she was dead. Surely to God it was not too much to ask, to send somebody 150 miles and back to get her what she wanted.

Eventually it was agreed that, so long as the volunteer travelled third class, the prison would fund the trip out of the money put aside for last requests. The volunteer went home to change. She knew there was a Cydrax bottle in the pantry which had a screw-in stopper. She found it and rinsed it out with boiling water, several times, and again with Domestos, and again with several boilings, until she was satisfied that it was perfectly clean and odourless. She took the tube from Holloway Road to King's Cross and walked the couple of hundred yards to St Pancras where there would shortly be a train to Derby with a connection to Buxton.

It was a fine day. People seemed cheerful. The journey, especially the last leg through Ashbourne and the beginnings of the High Peak countryside, was a peaceful delight. The warder, coming in to Buxton, thought it odd for a small town in the hills to have two railway stations bang next to each other but doubtless there were queerer things in the world than that. She asked the way to the spring water and set off down the hill at a brisk pace. She had fifty five minutes between trains. First job was to get the water. Then, she would find a cafe and have a quick snack.

The water was easy. It poured, warmly, freely and plentifully, from a brass lion's head beneath a carving of a woman and a girl dressed in cloaks. The warder filled her bottle and walked a few yards to a bench where she could sit and take a cigarette. Her packet of Passing Clouds had been rather squashed in her jacket pocket during her journey but the cigarettes were still serviceable. She mused idly, for the thousandth time, on why those cigarettes purporting to be in the Turkish style were oval, while those of the Virginian family were round.

After the cigarette she went in search of food. None of the cafes seemed to be open. In fact, at Miller's Cafe where Michelle used to work, they had decided to close for the day before, the day of, and the day after the execution, and all the other cafes and fish and chip shops had followed suit. Nobody wished to seem to profit from Miller's being shut and all wanted to express in their own way the shock and horror which everyone in Buxton was feeling, whether in sympathy with the murderess' victims or the murderess herself, or both.

The prison warder wasn't aware of this and presumed it was half day closing or something. In any case, the station buffet would be open, as indeed it was. The warder sat at her table with her repast: a cup of tea, a cheese and tomato sandwich, and a shiny rectangular object claimed to be a vanilla slice. She knew that the Labour government intended to nationalise the railways in the New Year. She hoped most sincerely that this would result in a significant improvement in the strength of the tea, the pliability and moistness of the bread, the flavour and quantity of the cheese and likewise of the margarine, the vulnerability of the vanilla slice to biting and chewing, and the all-round freshness of everything. This she fervently wished as she consumed her sustenance with an eye on the clock and an ear to the station announcer.

With only five minutes to go, she thought it peculiar that no announcement had been made about the train to Derby which she expected to catch, so she went to ask a porter. Oh no, that train, he told her, was Saturdays only at this time of year. There were no more trains to Derby until the six fifteen, which connected with the seven fifty two express to London, which would get her in to St Pancras at eight minutes past ten.

The warder was in a panic. Was there any other way? Was there a bus to Derby? She had to be in London before that. She knew the governor, a stickler. He wouldn't bend any rules, lights out, supper time, anything, not even for a last request. She really ought to be there by eight at the latest.

The porter did all he could, involving the assistant station master and the woman in the ticket office. Various options were discussed - Miller's Dale and Chesterfield for one, Manchester for two, the bus to Derby, but none offered much improvement on the six fifteen. The warder thanked them, asked where the telephone was and checked her purse for change. Two pennies and a shilling would surely be enough.

The operator put her through to the prison and the prison switchboard put her through to the governor's office. There was, said the governor, no question of waiting until eleven at night to give Michelle her water, which was the time it would be after the warder had tubed and walked from the station. Lights were out at nine. What, then, asked the frantic warder, about giving it to her in the morning? No, no, last requests were to be enjoyed and savoured the night before, not knocked back in an instant between stages in a most inflexible and inexorable process. At any rate, the chaplain and the Sheriff of the County would be there, with various other dignitaries. A High Court judge would be there. Eveything was timed to the most precise degree. No, no, it wasn't possible. We could not take the slightest risk with such a cast-iron procedure for the sake of a glass of water. They would just have to give her a glass of London's best draught H2O tonight and hope she didn't notice.

The warder, a woman of mature years and substantial build, her natural defences almost perfectly fortified by a long career dealing with some of the most unfortunate and some of the most wicked of women, put the receiver back on its hook and wept. Someone coming to use the telephone and about to knock on the glass, stayed his hand when he saw the large, middle-aged woman inside the box, her body bent and shaking, her forearm against the box wall and her forehead resting on it, and the tears visible as they fell to the floor. The man walked away and asked if there was another telephone box handy.

"Are you sure this is all you want?" said a warder to Michelle at about seven that evening, offering a glass of water. This was a warder Michelle knew, but one who had been on other duties most of the time since she'd come on at two. She'd been told to take this glass to the condemned cell, and that was all she was told.

"Thank you" said Michelle, with a half smile. "Nothing else, thank you. Have you just come on? Sylvia, isn't it? Will I see you in the morning?"

Sylvia shook her head, unable to speak, and turned away. She managed to close the door behind her and lock it before she burst into tears, but it was a near thing. Inside the condemned cell, Michelle looked at her water.

At about this time, the warder's train was approaching Derby with its now useless cargo of one bottle of Buxton spring water, and Ernest Mycock was in the gypsy caravan looking, with a tear stained face, at the equally deflated Gitana. She had made them some supper on her beautiful stove - a rabbit stew with onions, potatoes and carrots - and the two of them had just finished making a desultory effort at eating it. They were too tired. They had exhausted their ideas and themselves in their efforts to have Michelle reprieved and now there was nothing left to do. After a while they cuddled up on the bed and fell asleep.

After the arrest for the Stride murder, five more bodies which had suffered the same modus operandi were discovered at the spot. Up to and during the trial, which had considerable coverage in the newspapers, and right to the time of the verdict, nobody believed Michelle was sane except herself and one other. Michelle refused to plead insanity. She insisted on not guilty, since the homicides she had committed had been justified.

The trial was held at the Old Bailey rather than the Derby Crown Court, because of its national importance and to ensure a fair process of law without local bias, but on the evidence any jury would have been forced to find her guilty of murder. Michelle's twelve good men and true of London, rather than Derby, were no surprise in that respect. They did make a strong recommendation for clemency on the grounds of mental derangement, which was completely ignored by the one other who believed in Michelle's sanity, the judge.

This long-faced Solomon in a wig was a man for whom all forms of mental illness were a fiction. He had been a young army officer at the end of the First World War. His view then was that shell shock was a malingering pretence put up by the inferior spirits of the working class and now, as a judge in the principal criminal court in the land, his view on the possible derangement of murderers was identical. Nor did it occur to him that the judicial killing of a young girl, no matter what crimes she had committed, might be considered barbaric in some quarters. If such a thought had indeed occurred, he would have taken it as a warning of impending feeble-mindedness and senility, to be contemptuously dismissed.

His demeanour as he placed the black silk square on his head was that of a god automaton. What had been done was done, and here was the consequence. When sentencing a murderer there was, in essence, no real requirement for intervention by a human being. Admittedly, the machine had yet to be invented which could pronounce a death sentence and so someone was needed to give voice to society's vengeance. Without an automatic, mechanical death sentencer, this judge would have to step in and, as soon as he heard the word 'Guilty' from the foreman of the jury, reach for his black cap.

Unlike many of his courtroom colleagues, this judge had taken the trouble to find out what actually happened when a person was hanged, and he had attended the execution of a number of those men he had sentenced to that fate. In no way did his research nor his witnessing amend his feelings on the subject. He viewed the act of execution as a straightforward, perfectly natural and uncontroversial result of a murder conviction. He was more satisfied in himself to see at first hand that the objective of hanging in Great Britain was not to strangle the victim or give him a painful and unpleasant death, wriggling and dancing without dignity. In Great Britain, death was quick and clean. The law did not seek to inflict torture but simply to dislocate or fracture the first three cervical vertebrae thus damaging fatally and instantaneously the vital centres in the spinal cord.

This was achieved by placing a noose around the neck, generally with the knot behind the ear although it could also be under the chin, then allowing the condemned to fall, usually a distance of between six and eight feet depending on the weight of the person. Too little a drop and the vertebrae may not be sufficiently dislocated. Too much, and the head might be pulled right off. This was the skill of the hangman, who was possibly the only member of the working class whom the judge admired. A good hangman didn't need to weigh his subject in order to calculate the length of the drop. A good hangman simply eyed the subject up and down and made an educated and accurate estimate.

Oh yes, this judge had a considerable reputation based on his views and his knowledge. At the Carlton Club he might have been a bore had his conversation not had such a gruesome fascination about it. He told anyone who would listen, and many who would not, that the duty of execution fell upon the sheriff of the county in which it was to take place, and that a public notice of the date and hour of execution must be posted on the wall of the prison twelve hours before the appointed time and must stay there until the inquest was completed.

At the execution, those required to be present were the sheriff, the gaoler, the chaplain and the prison surgeon. And the condemned man, of course! This was the judge's only known joke. The surgeon completed the death certificate and the sheriff signed a declaration to the effect that sentence of death had been carried out. The coroner held an inquest on the body, and that was it. Off we jolly well went to the next case.

The way to get the judge really fired up in the bar, or after dinner in the club snorer, was to ask him what he thought about Sweden, for example, where the death penalty had been abolished in 1910. The judge, after some derogatory remarks about Swedes, would admit that the law in Great Britain could be more liberal. We could, for instance, follow the example of certain States in America, such as Utah, where the condemned were offered the choice of hanging or shooting.

After the verdict was passed on Michelle, there was no doubt in the country that she should be reprieved. Only those to do with the process of reprieving thought otherwise. Every official on every step up to the Home Secretary could not have been more unhelpful. The Home Secretary himself saw no reason to meddle in the affair. The newspapers made some attempts to soften the important hearts but they were easily distracted by causes with more likelihood of success.

Eventually, one commentator wrote that Michelle Mercer must be quite mad, 'a tortured soul living in an unbearable nightmare', and as such should be put out of her misery. This same worthy Fleet Street hack also pointed out that the mother had run away to America with a black airman and was not bothering to sail back across the Atlantic for a last meeting with her daughter. 'If the mother doesn't care, why should we?' seemed to be the implication. If the newspaper reporter knew that Michelle had written to her mother, pleading with her not to come, he didn't see fit to mention it.

All of this seemed like a convenient line to take so most of the newspapers now took it. It was a kind of 'We are so sorry, but...' which allowed them to stay on the moral mountain without annoying anybody or committing themselves to one side or the other. The great British public protested less and less. Gradually the flame of interest smouldered and smoked and went out, almost everywhere. The cause was lost. It was given up. No interests could be served by continuing even to discuss it. It was time to move on.

On the morning of the execution, a while after dawn had broken around the little caravan, Gitana awoke, made tea and took some to the still sleeping Ernest.

"Ernest" she said. "When this is over and we have begun our recovery, you will come to live with me in my caravan. We shall go on the road. You will cease to be a clerk. You will become a Romany. You will dress with a swagger, you will learn about horses and dealing and how to cheat the gorgio out of his antiques and jewellery, and you will write a book about our experiences. What do you say?"

"I think it's a wonderful idea. Are you sure I'm brave enough for it?"

"Quite sure. And the children can sleep in the cupboard under the bed."

Gitana went to the chest of drawers with a lightness in her feet and a glimmer in her heart.

"See here" she said. "A new luxury. Or, at least, a second-hand luxury. A wireless set! I have run a wire for the aerial out of the window and we are powered by a 12-volt accumulator which is slung underneath the van. My wireless here, which cost ten shillings and a palm reading, takes three minutes to warm up, but after that it's as good as can be."

Gitana turned the switch and went back to sit on the bed with Ernest, ready to listen to a voice of authority.

"This is the BBC Home Service. Here is the news and this is Alvar Liddell reading it. At six o'clock this morning, the condemned murderer Michelle Mercer was found dead in her cell. The cause of death is unknown but foul play is not suspected. Mercer was due to be executed at eight o'clock and the prison authorities are conducting the most urgent enquiries. In one of their first official meetings since their appointments, the Viscount Mountbatten, Governor-general of India, and Mr Jinnah, Governor-general of Pakistan, have..."